SEASONABLE DOUBT

A Cass Leary Legal Thriller

ROBIN JAMES

Seasonable Doubt

A Cass Leary Legal Thriller

By

Robin James

Chapter 1

HE SLID TWO SLENDER, white envelopes across the table. One in front of me, the other to the woman on my right. Her fingers trembled when she picked up hers. Odd, that. But then she'd been acting strange all day.

I caught her dabbing her eyes with a tissue as she sat in her car, waiting to pick me up from my motel. She'd been distracted, almost missing the turn to the title office in the heart of downtown Helene, Michigan. A quaint little resort town at the top of the mitten on the shores of Lake Michigan, between Petoskey and Charlevoix. A town that had only two intersections with traffic lights, and she blew through both of them.

"Are you okay?" I'd asked her. She said she was. But this wasn't the shark I'd dealt with for the last few months. The woman who'd negotiated this sale with a spine made of steel. Aimee Whittaker, Northern Michigan's top-selling realtor for five years running.

"Aimee?" the title agent said. His name was Dwayne. An affable guy. He'd inherited the business from his father who'd inherited it from his grandfather.

"I'm sorry," Aimee said, forcing a smile.

"You wanna check the amount?"

I slid a fingernail under the envelope flap and pulled out my check.

It was big. More zeros than I'd seen in a while. Aimee's check, I knew, coming in the last two weeks of the year would ensure she got another top-earner plaque to hang in her office.

"I trust you, Dwayne," Aimee said. She slipped her check into her purse. Dwayne shot me a look. I'd only met him today, but clearly, he realized Aimee's behavior had me concerned as well.

"Thanks, Dwayne," Aimee said, her voice breaking. She was about to start crying. Right there in the middle of what had to be one of her largest house closings of the year.

There was something going on. Dwayne moved in and whispered something in her ear. It seemed an intimate gesture. Of course, these two had worked together hundreds of times, probably thousands. I suddenly felt like an intruder even though it was my money giving both of them their Very Good Year.

"I'm just going to step outside for a minute," I said.

Dwayne quickly slipped into the chair I'd just vacated and brought his head close to Aimee's. She was falling apart right in front of us.

I stepped out into the hallway. Classical Christmas music played softly from speakers in the lobby. A white Christmas tree flickered in the corner, decorated with blue and silver bulbs all bearing the title company's logo. Window-cling menorahs festooned the glass double doors leading to the street.

I slipped my giant check into my bag, feeling a little like Santa Claus with it. The proceeds of this sale would keep roofs over my brothers' and sister's heads for the rest of their lives. It would help me start college funds for my nieces and nephews that came along. I'd do something special for the people who helped keep my law practice going, Jeanie Mills and Miranda Sulier. I had to be careful though. They both hated extravagances.

"We didn't think that house would ever go on the market again."

Dwayne's receptionist looked up from her computer screen, flashing me a bright smile.

"I'm sorry?"

"The Endicott house," she said. "On the point. It had been vacant for over a decade. A shame, really. Are you familiar with the history of the house?"

A lump formed in my throat. I knew she meant a different history than I had with the house. It seemed a lifetime ago when my former fiancé, Killian Thorne, bought it for us. A beautiful, four-thousand-square-foot Victorian home sitting on a private bluff overlooking Lake Michigan. He'd done it on a whim. Because I'd casually mentioned I wanted to retire up north. Being from Ireland, not Michigan, he didn't realize that the phrase "up north" meant something entirely different to Michiganders. We don't mean the literal north of the state. It's more nebulous and depending on where you live, "up north" can mean anything north of Lansing all the way to the Upper Peninsula.

"I'm familiar with some of it," I said.

"Oh, the Endicott was built in 1875," she said. "Did you know that? The Endicott family owned it that whole time until the last one of them died fifteen years ago. And then you bought it. The Endicotts rented it out for weddings and fundraising events for most of the last half of the twentieth century. I miss that. My parents got married there."

"Ah," I said. "Well, I can't say I know much about the new owners. Only that their check cleared." I patted the outside compartment of my bag.

"Sure," the receptionist said. I stepped a little closer. Her desk nameplate read Wanda. "Still, we get a little worried around here with newcomers."

I raised a brow. "Seems to me Helene wouldn't exist without newcomers. You've got a whole tourism industry that depends on it."

Helene had some of the cleanest, most pristine sand beaches along the coveted shoreline just west of Little Traverse Bay. More secluded than Petoskey or Charlevoix, the place was a boutique vacation destination.

"Lord," Wanda said. "I didn't mean it all snooty like that. I just mean I hope the new owners don't do anything weird with that house. I mean, not that the zoning board would let them. They do a good job protecting us out here."

"Of course," I said. I might have said more, but Aimee and Dwayne came out of the conference room just then. Her face was purple, her eyes bloodshot. Dwayne had his arm around Aimee. She blew her nose into a hanky then found a smile for me as she came around the reception desk.

"I owe you lunch," she said brightly.

"You don't have to do that," I said. "I've actually already checked out of my hotel. I should probably hit the road. It's a five-hour drive back to Delphi."

"Maybe you can spare at least five minutes for our Aimee," Dwayne said. He gave her a nudge in my direction. Dwayne clearly wanted Aimee to talk to me about it.

Now even Wanda had an expectant look on her face. She gave Aimee a nearly imperceptible nod. I had the distinct feeling I was about to be ambushed.

"I suppose I have some time," I said. "I was hoping to get home before dark. I need to turn in my rental car. And there's some weather coming ..."

Then, Aimee Whittaker, the most ruthless realtor in northern Michigan, started to cry in earnest.

"Please," Wanda and Dwayne said.

"You can use the conference room," Dwayne said. "I'll send out for lunch."

"Okaaay," I said.

Dwayne ushered Aimee back into the conference room. I followed her. Dwayne closed the door behind us, and Aimee practically collapsed into a chair.

"I think maybe you better tell me what's going on," I said. "Is it something with the house?" I knew Aimee was also representing the buyers. It was the other reason that commission check in her purse should have made her smile, not cry.

She shook her head. "No. It's not that. It's ... I don't know what to do. Who else I should talk to? I feel terrible. You barely know me. We're not ... friends. And I thought I had all of this handled. I did. Then today ... it all just fell apart right before I picked you up."

"Okay," I said, taking a seat. "So what's going on? Are you in trouble?"

"It's not me. It's my cousin. Nick. He's ... Cass ... he's been accused of something awful. Just awful. It's all such a mess."

"Did he hurt someone?"

Aimee blew her nose into a tissue, then nodded. "Steve Anspaugh."

She said the name as if I should know who that was. When she saw my expression, she put her tissues down.

"They're saying Nicky beat Steve within an inch of his life. I mean, the literal inch of his life. With a tire iron. He's been in a coma for months. They're saying he'll probably never wake up. It's so terrible. He's got a wife. Nicky has nobody. He just has me. And now he doesn't even have a lawyer."

"You want me to talk to him?"

Aimee launched herself across the table and gathered my hands in hers. "Would you? Please? I wouldn't ask. But I thought I had it all handled. His lawyer just ... bailed on him. That's the phone call I got this morning just before we came. He's lost, Cass. Nicky's just lost. I know he didn't do this. I know what they're saying about that surveillance footage. But I just know this wasn't Nicky."

Oh boy, I thought. There was a video. Of course, there was a video.

"Just talk to him. That's all. I'm scared, Cass. Nick just has the biggest heart of anybody I've ever known. This is killing him. He won't ask for help. I had to force him to use the lawyer I got for him. And now ... he's just ... well, I'm afraid."

I should have said no. Helene County wasn't exactly in my backyard. I don't know what made me do it. They say I'm a sucker for lost causes. But as Aimee Whittaker cried against my shoulder, I found myself agreeing to meet with her cousin Nick. Then fifteen minutes after that, she drove me to the county jail where he was being held.

"Wait here," I told her as the deputies looked at my bar card and identification.

"Hey, Aimee," one of them said. "Hang in there. He seems better today."

This got a new round of tears from Aimee. Deputy Walling, a young kid, probably fresh out of college, led me down the hallway to the lawyer's room.

"I'll be outside," he said. "You can take all the time you need."

I thanked him and walked into the small, windowless room. I'd been in a million of these in my career. Drab brick walls painted beige. A long rectangular table with loops through the center for wrist irons.

I waited five minutes before the inner door opened and Deputy Walling led the inmate in. I had my face in my phone. When I looked up, the breath went straight out of me.

Inmates of the Helene County, Michigan jail were issued red jumpsuits with black lettering down the right pant leg. The man shuffling toward me had a thick head of white hair and a fluffy beard that hung to the center of his chest. He was large. Six feet at least and probably three hundred pounds, including a bulging belly that wobbled like jelly as he walked toward the table. I found a smile. I think I said my name. But there in front of me, in leg irons and handcuffs, was friggin' Santa Claus himself.

Chapter 2

"I KNOW WHAT YOU'RE THINKING," he said.

He had a round little nose that almost seemed too small for his face. He had high cheekbones with a permanent rosy glow. His ankle chains rattled as he took his seat across from me. Deputy Walling gave me a nod and gestured that he'd be right outside the door.

"I can assure you," I said. "You have no idea what I'm thinking. I don't even know what I'm thinking."

He dropped his chin to his chest, making his white beard hang even longer. It nearly touched the table top. It had a thick, luxurious wave to it rather than growing kinky like most beards do.

"Mr. Whittaker," I said. "I'm not entirely sure why I'm even here. I ..."

"Aimee's going out of her mind," he said. "She worries about me. She shouldn't."

"She said you're her cousin. She said you've been charged with attempted murder."

"I didn't do it," Whittaker said. His blue eyes seared through me. He was on the verge of tears.

"They all say that." It wasn't the kind of thing I normally said. There was nothing helpful about it. I was tired. It had been a long drive yesterday and I had another one in front of me. At this rate, it wouldn't make sense to get on the road until tomorrow morning anyway. I just hoped my little motel still had vacancies.

"I really didn't do it," he said.

"Mr. Whittaker ..."

"Nicholas," he said. "My name is Nicholas. Er ... Nick."

"Of course it is," I muttered. "Listen. I told your cousin I'd talk to you. She said you've lost your lawyer?"

"Mr. Gale," he said. "He was helping me out. Aimee raised a bunch of money to pay his fee. I did everything he said. He promised this would be over by now. Now he's just ... gone."

"He withdrew?"

"He's just gone. That's all I know. You can't help me. No one can help me. They're saying I hurt Mr. Anspaugh. I'd never hurt anybody."

"Okay. Why don't you start from the beginning? I'm at a loss here."

"Mr. Anspaugh," he said. "He works for the county. The zoning board. Everybody knows him. But everybody knows me too. They know me. I've never hurt a soul. I never would hurt a soul.

How can they think I could do what someone did to poor Mr. Anspaugh?"

"What happened?"

"It was just a party. A Christmas in July holiday party. They do it every year. A whole week of events. I set up my light show that week, too. I used to just start it after November 1st. It's a lot of work. But every single year for the last fifteen or so. The little kids, they call me the Christmas Guy when they see me out and about. I have a website and everything. The librarian asked me to come out to pose for pictures. I was in costume."

"As Santa Claus," I said.

He nodded. "It started out kinda small. Something I'd just do for the little kids in the family. My cousin's kids. Aimee's kids. But they're all grown now. Then other people started asking me to do it. You know, I always thought it made me weird that my hair went gray by the time I was thirty. Kids used to tease me about it. But later, when I got older and fatter, well, it just makes me happy seeing all those kids' faces light up. So I started going to events at the library. They hired me at the mall for pictures with Santa. Now I go all over. Parades. Store openings. Aimee helps me keep track of it all with this calendar. Last year I did over fifty events. And not all around Christmas. Like the party in July. I'm getting booked more and more, all year round."

"Okay. And you're saying this event at the library was the first one you did this year?"

"Yes. And the last one." His voice cracked. "I didn't know it would be that. It was just a quick one, too. Just in and out. Took some pictures with the little kids in front of the big tree they decorate in the library alcove. But I told them. I told Mr.

Anspaugh I couldn't stay long. I had to be out of there by nine thirty so I could get home and make my appearance by ten."

"Your appearance?"

"I told you, I do a light show. See, that started out little too. I was an electrician before I hurt my back. I started building these Christmas light sets in front of my house. Reindeer. Snowmen. Christmas trees. A sleigh. All in colorful LED lights. I've got it set up on a computer program. If you drive out there and turn your radio to 107.2 on your FM dial, it's set to Christmas classics. It's a big draw. And I go out there in my Santa suit and wave. Every night at nine during the holiday season. But that night it was ten because it was July. Because we had to wait for it to get dark. So I told the librarian I had to be out of there by nine thirty. She said it was fine. She said they understood."

"What happened to Mr. Anspaugh?" I asked.

Nick Whittaker wouldn't look me in the eye. That didn't bode well.

"He was fine the last time I saw him. We spoke. He thanked me for being there. But I was in a hurry. I told Mrs. Connor, the librarian. I was worried because there were still about twenty kids waiting to have their picture taken after nine. I didn't want to disappoint them. But I didn't want to disappoint the kids waiting for me back at the house, either."

"For the light show."

"Right. I feel so bad. Aimee says they're still coming out. She made sure to set everything up. It's all on the computer. I showed her what to do a few years ago. I had the flu and she helped me. So at least the kids are still getting the show every night. They're just not getting me."

"But what about Steven Anspaugh? What evidence do they have against you regarding his assault?"

Whittaker shook his head. "It wasn't me. I'm telling you. But they have a videotape. They're saying I followed Mr. Anspaugh out to the parking lot at nine thirty."

"But they have surveillance footage? From the parking lot?"

He nodded. "It looks like me. I'm not saying it doesn't look like me. If I didn't know ... I mean ... If I had gone out there with him, I would have said sure, that's me. But it wasn't, because I didn't go out that way. I didn't follow Mr. Anspaugh. And I certainly didn't hurt him."

"What did your last lawyer say? Mr. uh ... Gale, was it?"

"He said this wouldn't even go to trial. He said they wouldn't be able to prove their case. But then ... they found that tire iron."

"Where?"

"They said it had Mr. Anspaugh's blood all over it. They found it near my trash can. I'm telling you. I didn't put it there. I don't even know how to use a tire iron. And now ... all these people. They said they liked me. Said they loved me. But they've turned, Ms. Leary. I don't understand it. I don't understand why all these people are saying I wanted to hurt Mr. Anspaugh. I didn't. I'm telling you. I didn't. We didn't always agree, but it was respectful. You know?"

"What did you disagree about?"

"Everybody had issues with him. He doesn't like newcomers. New businesses. People changing things. He's afraid of it."

The words of Wanda, the receptionist at the title agency echoed in my mind. They don't like newcomers in Helene.

"You said Anspaugh works for the zoning board?"

"He's on the zoning board, yes. He's the most influential member of it. What he says goes, pretty much."

As Whittaker said it, it jogged something in my memory. The Endicott house was part of the historical register. I believe I had a letter or two bearing Anspaugh's signature regarding restrictions the township might place on renovations I had at one time wanted to make.

"Let me guess," I said. "Mr. Anspaugh didn't like your light show."

"It wasn't that he didn't like it. Everybody likes it. Even my neighbors. I make sure of that. The pastor across the street even lets people park in his lot so they can see it. The church has been letting me do that for years. People get mad though. Not about my stuff. They get mad at each other. See, you gotta turn off your headlights or it makes it harder for people to see my lights."

"Sure."

"He was gonna vote for me, I know it. I could just tell."

"Vote for you?"

"There was gonna be a vote in front of the zoning board. A couple of people complained. Anonymous. Can you believe that? If they'd have just come and talked to me one-on-one. But the board was gonna vote on whether I could keep the show going. I needed a special variance. All of a sudden. I mean, I've been doing that light show for fifteen years, Ms. Leary. Why all of a sudden now somebody raises a stink?"

"So let me get this straight. The case against you ... they've got you on videotape following the victim out to the parking lot. They've got a bloody weapon they pulled from your garbage. And Steven Anspaugh was the man standing between you and the light show you've put on for the town for fifteen years?"

"And they said I wasn't where I said I was. They say I've got no alibi."

"Which was what?"

"I went home," he said. "I'm telling you. I just went home. I had to get back so I could come out and wave at all the people watching the show. It's kind of the finale. I come out in the suit. It's right at the end of Jolly Old Saint Nicholas. You know. The song."

"I do indeed."

"And the lights on the roof. I've got reindeer going all the way up and an LED chimney. Rudolph's nose lights up at the very end. That's the big finish."

"Were you out there at ten? People can confirm that?"

"He wasn't working. Rudolph wasn't working. I got an error message. I was trying to figure out what had happened. So I was late."

"How late?" I said, my stomach sinking.

"I don't know. Fifteen. Twenty minutes."

The gears of my mind shifted. I'd have to see the timestamps on the surveillance footage myself, but I'd bet they'd reveal a substantial gap between the last time Whittaker appeared on screen in that parking lot and when he showed up in front of a line of cars at a light show.

"Can you help me? Will you help me? Will you take a look at my case?"

"Mr. Whittaker, I'm not from Helene. I don't ..."

"That's why you're perfect. Mr. Gale? He's from Helene and that hasn't helped me one bit. He abandoned me. And my trial's next week."

"But you don't have a lawyer. Surely the judge has to know that. You could seek a continuance."

"I don't know how."

"You ask the judge. You file a motion."

"I don't know how to do any of that. Mr. Gale said it would never get this far."

It was then he started to cry. It was unsettling, to say the least. This big, burly man was reduced to tears. Something about it tugged at me.

I didn't make a conscious decision to get out of my chair. But I found myself standing next to him. Then Nick Whittaker wrapped his arms around me and sobbed into my sleeve.

"I wanted to do something good," he said. "I thought I was doing something good. But they all turned on me. Or a lot of them, anyway. I swear to you. I didn't hurt Mr. Anspaugh. Someone else did this. It wasn't me. I can't fight this by myself. I don't know what to do. Aimee said maybe you would help. She said you're good at this. She said you're nice."

Nice. I don't know why the word made me want to burst out laughing. It was like Santa Claus himself was trying to put me on the nice list. This felt surreal.

"They're saying I could be in here for the rest of my life. If Mr. Anspaugh never wakes up. He's been in a coma all this time, Ms. Leary. I feel terrible for his family. To have him in the hospital like that, hooked up to all those machines. On Christmas."

And to think of Nick Whittaker, er ... Santa Claus, in lock-up on Christmas too.

"You're here," he said. I handed him a tissue. He blew his nose and the sound of it, like a strangled goose, echoed through the room. "Mr. Gale hasn't been returning my calls."

"Well, the judge needs to know that," I said. "If what you're saying is true ..."

"It's true. I swear it on my life. I'm telling you the truth. I didn't hurt Mr. Anspaugh."

"Well, if your lawyer has abandoned you on the eve of trial, that's certainly grounds for adjourning your trial until after the holidays."

"I don't want that!" he said. "No. I have to get out of here. I can't be here on Christmas Eve. I have things to do!"

I resisted the urge to say something sarcastic about delivering toys. The second I thought it, my heart sank to my shoes. Nick Whittaker looked so lost and broken as he sat across from me.

You and your lost causes, I could almost hear my law partner, Jeanie Mills, whispering in my ear.

There was a soft knock on the door and Deputy Walling stuck his head back in. "I'm sorry to cut you short. But we need the room. Are you finished?"

"Yes," I said, rising.

"Will you help me? Please?"

I tried to find a smile for the man. "I can't make you any promises. But I'll see what I can do."

His shoulders sagged with relief. "Thank you. I knew you were one of the nice ones."

My step faltered. I looked back at Nick Whittaker. A bit of joy came back into his face as I said my goodbye and stepped out into the hall.

Chapter 3

"Walk away from this one, Cass."

I chewed on the end of a pen. Jeanie's smiling face from the photo I took of her last Christmas looked back at me from my phone screen as I talked to her on speaker.

"You should see this guy," I said. "Straight out of North Pole central casting. And he seems earnest enough. The case is pretty straightforward. I'm waiting to hear back from the prosecutor."

"You already talked to the prosecutor? Cass, that means you're already in this. You're not just kicking the tires, are you?"

"His lawyer abandoned him. That's actually the reason I wanted to run all this by you. One of them anyway. It's gotta be a coincidence. At least I thought it was. But the bar numbers match. His defense lawyer of record is E. Thomas Gale."

"Gale Force?" she asked. "Hmm."

"What do you mean, hmm?"

"E. Thomas Gale. The guy who repped Dr. Anton Milo? You know they made a movie out of that? *Deadly Affair*. Cass, he made legal punditry sexy back in the nineties. During the OJ trial. He was one of the most sought-after commentators. He made a second fortune. What's a guy like that doing up in nowhere, Michigan?"

"I don't know. But more to the point, what's a guy like that doing abandoning his client on the eve of trial? The week before Christmas? I can't get a straight answer out of anybody."

"Well, what do you know?"

"I know there's supposed to be a videotape of Santa ... er ... Nick Whittaker following the victim across the parking lot. A few minutes later, he supposedly is seen walking back alone carrying a tire iron in his hand. I'm waiting to get a copy of the tape."

"Hmm. You really wanna commit yourself to a whole trial all the way up there?"

"No. Not at all. And I'm not. But maybe I can at least file a motion for this guy, get his trial pushed back. Help him get a new lawyer."

"You're not coming back tonight, are you?"

I tapped my pen against the side of my chair. "There's a final pretrial scheduled for tomorrow morning in front of a Judge Vince Homer. Hopefully, he'll be reasonable. It'll be in and out and then I'll hit the road."

"What do you need from me?" Jeanie asked.

I smiled. She would argue with me until I made up my mind about something. Then she'd be my ride or die.

"Nothing yet. And I'm not saying I'm taking this case. I'm just making sure this poor guy isn't left to his own devices. That's all."

"Hmm."

"That's your third hmm, Jeanie."

"Stop counting."

"I'll be back in the office tomorrow evening," I assured her. "The day after tomorrow at the latest. I know you can hold the fort down for me."

"You're days from Christmas, Cass. You're supposed to be on vacation. You promised me you'd take a breather."

"And I will."

There was a knock on my hotel room door. I checked the time on my phone. It was after nine o'clock at night.

"I'll call you in the morning after the hearing," I said. "Let you know my ETA."

"All righty," Jeanie said. "Just be careful not to get sucked too far down this rabbit hole."

"Bah humbug," I teased. I clicked off the call and went to the door. I peered through the peephole. Aimee Whittaker stood there with a thick file folder under one arm.

I opened the door. "Everything okay?"

Aimee gave me a weak smile. She'd carefully applied her makeup, but I could tell she'd been crying again.

"I'm sorry to bother you," she said. "But this just couldn't wait until tomorrow morning. I knew you'd want all of this as soon as I got my hands on it."

I opened the door wider and gestured for her to come inside. My room wasn't much. Just a standard with a queen-sized bed. I hadn't intended to stay here longer than one night. There was just a small round table in the corner. I had my laptop on it next to my cell phone. I scooped those up as Aimee sat down and plopped the file folder on the table.

"His secretary dropped all this off at my office about an hour ago," she said. "She swears it's all he has."

"He?"

"Mr. Gale," she said. "I've been trying to get a hold of him for two weeks. So has Nick. When I told his secretary you talked to Nick, she had this sent over right away."

"What is it?" I asked, then instantly regretted it. Aimee opened the flap on the file and pulled out a single page. It was an affidavit signed by none other than E. Thomas Gale.

"Aimee, I haven't said whether ..."

"She said all you have to do is file this with the judge tomorrow."

I took the paper from her hand. It was a motion for substitution of attorney. E. Thomas Gale, or someone acting for him, had written my name on the bottom of the form.

"So he's actually dumping Nick, a week before trial. Aimee, that's not exactly ethical. I could even argue that it's malpractice."

Aimee's eyes went wide. "Don't. Oh. Please. Don't do that. Look, I don't know what's going on with Mr. Gale. He's gotten a bit ... um ... eccentric over the years. But he's a legend around here."

"He's a legend everywhere. That's why I'm completely mystified why he'd leave Nick hanging like this."

"Mr. Gale has done a lot for this community. He's invested a ton of money into local businesses. The downtown beautification committee."

"I'd like to speak to him," I said. I had two unreturned phone calls to his office already.

"He's not taking calls," Aimee said. "That much I can tell you for sure. His secretary told me that."

"Well, then I'll just have to go see him."

"You probably won't be able to do that easily either. Gale lives out on an island in the middle of the bay. You'd need a boat to get out there."

"A boat? In December?"

"This is what I'm saying."

"Unbelievable. Well, I'll just have to bring this all up to Judge Homer tomorrow. There's just no way, under the circumstances, Nick's trial can go forward as scheduled."

Deep lines of worry creased Aimee's face. My words didn't seem to bring her any relief.

I pulled out the first stack of paper from the file folder. There seemed to be no logical organization to Thomas Gale's file. There were letters to and from him to the prosecutor, Lucas Braunlin. It looked like he'd asked for an adjourned trial date once before and got it. I skimmed more papers until I found a copy of the full police report. It was close to an inch thick. In it were photographs of the victim, Steven Anspaugh.

"My God," I whispered. These had been taken at the hospital. His face was barely recognizable as human. His eyes were blackened, swollen, several of his teeth were missing.

"He hasn't regained consciousness as far as you know?" I asked.

Aimee shook her head. "No. They kept him in a medically induced coma for the first few weeks. They were worried about the swelling on his brain."

I put the photographs down. Swelling on the brain. Not too long ago, I'd sat beside my assistant Tori's hospital bed after she'd been injured in a car accident. Though she hadn't looked this bad, the injuries were similar.

"If he dies," I said, "they can upgrade Nick's charges to murder."

A tear fell from Aimee's eyes. "I know he didn't do this, Cass. I thought Mr. Gale was going to be able to prove that. He promised."

I swallowed the retort I wanted to make. He shouldn't have promised.

"Well," I said. "It's not his job to prove Nick is innocent. It's this Braunlin's job to prove he's guilty."

"Do you think he can?"

"I don't know enough of anything yet. Let me just get through tomorrow's pretrial for him. Then I'll help you find a defense lawyer who can represent him at trial."

Aimee looked like she was going to say something else. Instead, she found a faint smile.

"Thank you. For everything. For anything, really. I hope you get a chance to get to know Nick. I know he might seem odd to you. He is. But he's mine, you know? My dad and his dad were brothers. Nick's always been kind of a loner. Never had a lot of self-confidence. Growing up he didn't really date. Didn't really ever fit in anywhere. Then, I don't know. He kind of fell into this role as the Christmas Guy. Did he tell you that's what some of the kids call him?"

"He did."

"It has saved him, Cass. Gave him a purpose. His parents? My aunt and uncle. They were always so worried about what would happen to Nick after they were gone. He lived with them until they both finally passed. They made us promise. All of us cousins. Make sure we invite Nicky over. Check on him. They were worried he'd have nowhere to go on holidays. On Christmas. Now, in this town? He is Christmas."

I reached across the table and put my hand on her shoulder. "I'll do what I can," I reassured her. I just prayed my good deed wouldn't go unpunished.

Chapter 4

"YOUR HONOR," Lucas Braunlin said as he stepped up to the lectern in Courtroom Number One of the Helene County Circuit Courthouse. Judge Vince Homer leaned to one side of his chair, twirling the end of his readers as Braunlin spoke.

"This court has generously agreed to push back Mr. Whittaker's trial twice already. Mr. Anspaugh's family, the people of this county, and the State of Michigan deserve to see justice served. I know I don't need to remind the court of the severity of Mr. Anspaugh's injuries, the brutality of this crime, or the tremendous amount of taxpayer resources that have already been devoted to this case."

"Taxpayer resources?" I muttered. Judge Homer looked my way. Braunlin stepped away from the lectern to make way for me.

"Ms. Leary?" Judge Homer said. Homer was an old school judge, I'd been told. The longest-serving member of the county bench. Aimee told me he was planning to finally retire after the first of the year. It meant Nick Whittaker's case would be the last trial of his career.

"Your Honor, it is my understanding that the defendant has been, in effect, without access to adequate counsel for several weeks."

"He has a lawyer," Braunlin said from his table. "A damn good one."

I looked back. Nick Whittaker sat hunched over at the defense table. Every time Braunlin spoke, Nick seemed to be trying to make himself smaller.

"Yes," I said. "However, Mr. Gale has been unreachable by Mr. Whittaker, by myself, for some time. I'm asking for an adjournment of his trial date until such time as he can secure a new defense attorney ..."

"He has," Judge Homer said. He picked up a piece of paper and waved it in the air. "He picked you. Mr. Gale has filed his motion for substitution. I have it right here."

"He what?" I muttered. "Your Honor, with all due respect, I've never even spoken to Mr. Gale. He hasn't returned my calls."

"Don't think he needs to," the judge said. "He's tagged you, Ms. Leary. You're it."

"I'm it? Your Honor, even if I'd agreed to take this case, would you really expect me ... Mr. Whittaker ... to have only a week to prepare for trial?"

"It's been almost six months," Homer said.

"Not for me, it hasn't. Look, I don't know what's going on with Thomas Gale ..."

"Then you'd be well advised not to speculate, Ms. Leary," the judge said. He sat up straight in his chair. "Mr. Gale is a revered member of the bar and citizen of this town."

"I'm not saying ..."

"I would think not. Now we are on the docket for next week. Are you prepared to proceed, Mr. Braunlin?"

"I am more than prepared."

"Mr. Whittaker," Judge Homer said. "Do you want this lady, Ms. Leary, to be your lawyer?"

"Yes, Judge. I'd like that a lot," Nick said.

"But ..." I started.

"Fine," Homer interrupted me. "So would the court. Ms. Leary, you have quite the reputation as a skilled trial lawyer. How many criminal trials have you defended?"

"What? I'm ... I can't say off the top of my head."

"Hundreds?"

"Um ... yes."

"You've won most of those, haven't you?"

I couldn't believe what he was asking me. This could not be real. He could not be about to do what I thought he was about to do.

"Most of them, yes. I don't exactly keep statistics."

"Ninety percent," the judge said. "You win ninety percent of the time. I'm not worried about your abilities, Ms. Leary. And I trust Mr. Gale's instincts as well. If he thinks you're ready to try this case, so do I."

"If he what?"

"Mr. Whittaker, are you asking to have your trial postponed again?" the judge asked.

"No, sir," Nick said. "I'd just as soon get on with it. I want to prove my innocence."

"That's not how this works," I said. "Your Honor ..."

"Defendant's motion to adjourn the trial date is denied," Judge Homer said. "We'll proceed with jury selection as scheduled, bright and early the morning of the 17th. Let's work hard to get this all wrapped up by Christmas Eve, shall we?"

"Of course, Your Honor," Braunlin said.

As my mouth dropped to the floor, Judge Homer banged his gavel and sealed my fate. Nick Whittaker beamed at me as I turned around and walked back to the table.

Chapter 5

I'D COVERED every square inch of the floor in the Helene Motel, Room 17 with boxes, paperwork, and file folders. In addition to the folder Aimee had brought me, E. Thomas Gale's office had sent over every other scrap of paper he had on Nick Whittaker's case. It came in the middle of the night by courier. Once again, every call I made to Gale himself went unreturned.

I opened my laptop and slipped Gale's flash drive into the port. It contained two.mp3 files. I opened the one labeled "the night in question."

"Okay then," I said to myself. I hit play.

After a few seconds of delay, the surveillance footage from the library parking lot came into view. The timestamp in the far right corner read nine seventeen.

The lot was full. At that time of day on July 25th, the sun hadn't fully set yet. I counted seven cars parked in various spots. There was a note in the police report listing every license plate and who they were registered to. Steve Anspaugh's black Lincoln Corsair was parked at the top of the frame.

At nine twenty-eight p.m., a man, presumably Anspaugh himself, came out the side door of the library. He had dark, thick hair and wore business casual that night. A white golf shirt with tan cargo pants. He turned, facing the door he'd just exited from. There was no audio on the playback, but he was gesturing with his hands, most certainly talking to someone as yet offscreen. Anspaugh had a medium build. I knew from the police report he was five foot nine and a hundred and seventy pounds. Trim, but not athletic. From his posture, he seemed angry, standing with his hands on his hips at one point, his chin and chest jutting out. He then made an exaggerated, dismissive gesture, waving someone off before he turned and walked toward his vehicle.

That's when a second figure walked into frame. My heart seized.

It was Santa Claus. Big, barrel-chested. That flowing white beard. He wore an ornate red costume with gold trim and a wide black belt, his boots polished to a shine, his Santa hat pulled low, just to the edge of his brow.

It certainly looked like Nick Whittaker. Same size. Same build. Same suit, of course, but this was a costume.

I paused the playback and tried to zoom in on his facial features. The image became hopelessly grainy. I knew the police had tried to enhance the footage but the distance of the camera and resolution provided little help. Plus, Santa's face was only in profile for a second or two before he walked toward Anspaugh and the camera could only pick him up from the back or briefly in profile.

My phone rang. Jeanie. I'd texted her last night after the hearing and filled her in on the highlights.

"Hi," I said, answering. I put her on speaker as I resumed playback on the library footage.

"He's insane," she said. "Judge Homer's lost his mind. He can't conscript you to handle a murder trial the week before Christmas."

"Attempted murder. And he has."

"You can file an interlocutory appeal."

"Who's going to hear it, Jeanie? It's the week before Christmas. Nobody's minding the store at the Court of Appeals this week."

"What about Gale?"

"Still AWOL. And I've gotten some pretty clear signals that it's a tree I shouldn't shake."

"What? Cass, he's committed malpractice. At the very least some pretty damning ethical violations that could get him disbarred."

"And none of that does Nick Whittaker any good. Homer's determined. He wants this trial to go forward. So does Whittaker. I'm outnumbered."

"I'll come up," she said.

"It won't help."

"It'll help you maybe."

"Jeanie, I need you where you are. Manning the fort so we aren't the ones abandoning our existing clients the week before Christmas."

She let out a deep sigh.

"Well, how does it look?"

I kept my eyes on my laptop screen. Anspaugh was walking briskly away from Santa Claus. He didn't seem aware he was being followed by him. But he didn't stop at his vehicle. Instead, he kept on walking around the building and out of view. I'd taken a drive out to the scene earlier today to get the lay of the land. There was a nature trail behind the library that led into five acres of mature woods. I'd been told it was a popular spot for photographs. Every bride, groom, prom, or homecoming dance attendees went out there for shots under the gazebo.

"I'm going to send you a copy of the surveillance footage," I said to Jeanie. "It's damning. It's just ..."

"What?" she asked. I cocked my head to the side. Now both Santa and Anspaugh were out of frame. I scrolled ahead in fifteen second increments. Finally, at nine fifty-two, Santa reemerged carrying a long, black, curved stick. I zoomed in. Not a stick. A tire iron. Again, his face was partially obscured by his hat and the angle he stood.

I right-clicked my mouse and saved a copy of the file on my hard drive, then quickly fired a copy off to Jeanie in an email attachment.

"There are witnesses who say they heard Whittaker and Anspaugh arguing at the Christmas in July party. It was heated. This footage, it really does appear Anspaugh's arguing with ... well ... Santa Claus. I'm just thinking ..."

"Thinking what, chief?" she said.

"He's in a costume, is all. You can't see his face. I feel like if this trial were happening anywhere else, I'd have reasonable doubt right there."

"Except they found the murder ... er ... attempted murder weapon in Whittaker's garbage."

"Yes."

"And Whittaker's alibi is full of holes."

"He swears he was back home by ten. It's a fifteen-minute drive from the library and this Santa is seen on video at nine fifty-two."

I clicked on a second video file. This one was a cell phone video taken in front of Whittaker's home the night of July 25th. It showed a few minutes of his impressive light show. Then, at ten twenty-seven, Santa-Whittaker emerged from his own front door to wave at the crowd.

"He's not where he says he was when he says he was there."

"He lied to the cops?"

"He says it wasn't intentional. He says he had technical difficulties with his light show that night that made him late getting out the front door but that he was home no later than nine forty-five."

"Except he's the only one saying it. And you've got video footage saying something very different. It's too convenient."

"It's too something all right."

"Cass, look. It's fishy. If you go to trial and a jury convicts Whittaker, he's got appealable error on his former lawyer's conduct alone."

"Maybe. But that'll take years to play out. Whittaker's family doesn't think he'll make it that long in prison."

"Does he have a record? Any past tendencies toward violence?"

"Nothing. By all accounts, up until last July, he was a sweet guy who enjoys dressing up as Santa Claus for the people of Helene. They loved him."

"Until they turned on him."

"Exactly."

"You said Anspaugh held the keys to whether he'd be able to keep doing his home light show?"

"That's the motive the prosecution is going to try to sell."

"Cass, if this guy's identity got wrapped up in being Santa. In getting the positive attention from that show ... don't you think he could get pretty angry and the thought of that being taken away from him."

"Of course. His cousin said he was devastated. Filled with worry pending the outcome of the zoning board's decision."

"And Anspaugh was leaning toward revoking his permission?"

"That's unclear. He never got a chance to vote. But I've heard from several people around here that Anspaugh was very anti-development."

"But this wasn't a development issue. What was his beef with Whittaker?"

"Still trying to figure that out too."

"What's the physical evidence?"

"The weapon was found with Anspaugh's blood on it in Whittaker's trash." I thumbed through the police report, re-reading it as I went.

"There were also synthetic fibers on Anspaugh's clothing consistent with the costume Whittaker was wearing."

"So he got close enough to him to transfer fibers?"

"Again, that alone shouldn't be enough to convict. I can blow holes through that. They were at the same party. I can use the prosecution's own argument against them. There's no dispute that Anspaugh and Whittaker were in close physical proximity to each other the night Anspaugh was attacked. One witness says she saw them arguing nose to nose. That Anspaugh actually poked Whittaker with a finger to the chest."

"You gotta be careful with that one. Because then you're also conceding the hostility between them."

"Right."

"What about Whittaker? You gonna put him on the stand?"

"I have no idea. I met him twice, Jeanie. I don't have a good gauge on how he'll stand up to cross."

"And you've got zero time. Ugh. Cass, I don't like this. It feels booby-trapped against you."

"It feels booby-trapped against Whittaker. That's the thing I can't shake. That's the thing that's keeping me from just telling Judge Homer to get bent and coming home."

"Well, you know I'm here for whatever you need. You want me to call Eric?"

"No," I said. "He's in North Carolina to be with his parents this year. If I call him with this ..."

"He's gonna get on a plane and get to you," she said.

"Exactly. I don't want to ruin anyone else's holiday plans over this. There's reasonable doubt just on the face of it."

"Razor thin," she said.

"That's all I need."

"Well, it's not all you need. But I take your point. Tell me what you want me to do?"

"The strongest pieces of evidence against Whittaker are the weapon and the fiber evidence from that costume. So I think I've got to find some way to make the jury doubt Whittaker was the one wearing it."

"Do you know where he gets them from?"

"I'm finding out," I said.

"Does he have more than one?"

"I'm finding that out too. It's distinct though. Just from this video footage, it looks ... well ... fancier than the ones you typically see on garden variety mall Santas. I need to ask Whittaker about it. I've got a meeting with him set up for the day after tomorrow."

"And the trial is scheduled in a few days. Jiminy Christmas, Cass."

"I know. I know."

"Will you let me do some digging into Gale too? It's got me thinking."

"How so?"

"Well, like I said. If you lose this thing, Whittaker's got appealable error. Ineffective assistance of his original counsel

coupled with Homer's boneheaded ruling substituting you in. I
never knew Tom Gale personally. But he was a rock star in his
prime, Cass. What if he figures this is his best way of helping
Whittaker? By opening the door for a solid appeal?"

"That," I said, "is the craziest strategy I've ever heard."

"But not implausible."

"Sure. Do some checking. For now, I've got to focus on winning
this thing for him."

"Ten-four," she said. "You know I've got your back if you need
it. What's next?"

"I'm headed over to Whittaker's house. His cousin is going to
meet me there this evening. And I want to walk the crime scene
again. I just drove by this morning to get a feel for it."

"It's gonna look different now with snow on the ground and no
leaves on the trees."

"I know. But I just need to get it in my head. The geography of
it all."

"Gotcha. Well, good luck saving Christmastown, Cass."

"Very funny. But thank you. I'm going to need it."

"I'll look at that surveillance footage and let you know if
anything pops out at me. If you figure out where he got those
costumes, let me know and I'll help you run that lead down too."

"Thanks, Jeanie. You're a lifesaver."

"I know."

I clicked off. As soon as I did, a text came through from Aimee
Whittaker.

"We're all set," she said. "I've got the keys to Nick's house. See you there at six."

I texted back an okay sign. On my laptop screen in front of me, I'd pressed pause. Nick Whittaker as Santa Claus smiled back at me with his white-gloved hand raised in a jolly wave.

Chapter 6

Six o'clock on December 15th and the sun had just begun to set. Nick Whittaker lived in a modest ranch house at the corner of Dover and Hill Road. They were two of the main streets in town. Helene High School, Junior High, and Elementary were just a mile down the road. The house faced a two-story church on the opposite corner, the Perpetual Hope Ministry. It had a flashy, LED sign out front displaying mass hours and pick-up times for its Christmas Break Bible School. Ten cars had already lined up in the parking lot, presumably waiting for the start of Nick Whittaker's light show.

Aimee had warned me to take the driveway where it curved around the back. I could see why. If I parked my rental car in front, it would block half of Nick's displays. Even darkened as they were now, it was an impressive installation.

He had at least fifty holiday-themed characters and iconography set up. Elaborately wrapped presents, elves, holly, snowmen, wreaths, snowflakes, and at the center, a giant pole maybe rising at least thirty feet up. There was a star at the top and dozens upon dozens of light strings tied to the ground around it. When lit, I could see it would create an impressive Christmas tree.

Aimee opened the back door and waved me in.

"You're just in time," she said. "Everything's set to go off in thirty minutes."

"He said he came in this way that night," I said, more to myself than to Aimee. This had been Nick's story. He came home after dark on July 25th, parked in the back so no one would see him. It was part of the illusion he said he liked to maintain. I wanted to get a better look from the parking lot across the street. Was it possible that no one saw him pull in?

"How long do they start lining up ahead of the show?" I asked.

I walked in the back door. It led to a galley kitchen with dark cabinets. Nick had green leather kitchen chairs around a round table that reminded me of one my Grandma Leary used to have. In fact, everything about this place was mid-century modern. He had white sugar and flour canisters on the counter right next to a Charles Chips container.

"I haven't seen one of these since I was a kid," I said, lifting the lid on the thing. There were no chips inside anymore. Just an assortment of rubber bands, paper clips, pens, and other flotsam one might normally throw in a junk drawer.

"Most of this belonged to his parents," Aimee said. "The house too. The control room's back here."

She led me through the kitchen and down a short hallway. It was a standard, three-bedroom ranch configuration. The largest bedroom Nick hadn't been using as his own. Instead, it was, as Aimee said, a control room. Nick had three computer monitors set up and a large tower PC in one corner.

"This is what runs everything? It looks old."

"I know," Aimee said. "Nick won't get a new one. He says they're too buggy. I don't know. He's set in his ways."

"Sure."

I went to the window. More cars had begun to pull into the church parking lot. Headlights lit up the room before I pulled the shades back down.

"That drives him nuts," Aimee said. "It's a lack of common courtesy. They're supposed to turn off their headlights to watch the show."

"Right. Sorry. I asked before. How far ahead of the show do they start lining up out there?"

"Oh, at least a half hour. People like to get those six spots right in front."

"It's a busy street," I said.

Aimee shrugged. "Busy for Helene, I guess. But most of the traffic is from two thirty to six when school's in session. After dinnertime it's pretty quiet."

I'd have to get a better look. But it seemed plausible that no one would have seen Nick pulling into his driveway from the side. Especially if he'd cut his headlights after he made the turn.

"I really don't even need to be here," Aimee said. "Nick's got everything on a timer. It's all automated. But it makes him feel better to know I'm here just in case something goes wrong."

"What if something goes wrong? Do you know how to troubleshoot it?"

"Not really. I mean, I can make sure the extension cords are plugged in. That's about it. But I don't have a clue how to run any of this software or fix a bug. It's just a small thing though. Me being here. If it makes him happy, then I'm happy to do it."

I came away from the window. There wasn't much in the room besides Nick's computer set-up and two leather gaming chairs. One was patched together with duct tape. I spotted his open closet door and went to it. Save for a few empty garment bags, there wasn't much in it.

"The cops took everything," Aimee said. "That's where Nick used to keep his Santa suits and boots."

I pushed each empty hanger back. In the very back of the closet, three black garment bags lay in a heap on the floor. I picked one up.

"He kept them so nice," Aimee said. "They just came in here and ripped through everything. Those suits aren't cheap. Nick paid thousands of dollars for them."

"They were custom-made?"

"I don't think custom. But he'd go to this shop down in Frankenmuth."

I saw a label sticking out of the plastic window in one of the bags. Jingle's Christmas Notions. There was a Frankenmuth address listed.

"Can I keep this?" I asked.

"Of course. Whatever you need."

I slipped the card in my pocket.

"It's almost time," Aimee said. "Let me just make sure everything starts up like it's supposed to. Then we can walk around back if you'd like. The best way to see it really is across the street."

"That's fine," I said. I walked out of Nick's control room and further down the hall. One bedroom looked like Nick was using it for storage. He had more Christmas decorations. Giant glittering reindeer. A few plastic candy canes as tall as I was. I walked back into the living room. The furniture in the front room was embroidered with green holly leaves. Two overstuffed chairs and a long couch. Each one covered in plastic. Again, just like my grandmother's house back in the eighties.

Nick had photographs hung all along the far wall. I stepped closer. Each picture was of Nick, dressed in his Santa regalia. Most of them were shots of him standing with entire groups of schoolchildren, their teachers beaming from the side. Another shot had Nick as Santa at a ribbon-cutting ceremony in front of the library. Another had him waving from a giant paper mache sleigh atop a parade float. Finally, I spotted one with Santa/Nick standing next to the last governor in front of the Mackinac Bridge.

A booming voice filled the room from a loudspeaker outside.

"Merry Christmas, one and all!" I jumped. Then the room was flooded with red and green light as the show outside began. "Joy to the World" played.

I walked back to the control room. Aimee stood in front of the monitor. "We're all good to go in here," she said. I could see different light zones on the monitor, all in the green indicating whatever program Nick had running was functioning as it should.

"How long will this run?" I asked.

"He has it go until eleven o'clock," she said. "So four hours during the dead of winter like this."

"How long did he have it running during the Christmas in July week?"

"Just an hour on that one. Nine to ten."

"And he'd come out for his ten o'clock wave."

"Right. He does that at nine and eleven during the holiday season proper. Except for this year, of course."

"Were you out there that night? Back in July?"

"No. I wish I had been. My youngest was sick that night. Otherwise, I would have taken him to the library party. I kick myself for that."

"You can't."

"Come on," Aimee said. She grabbed her coat off the back of the chair and led me back through the kitchen and side door.

We walked outside. I was temporarily blinded by the lights coming from the front yard. Aimee had me follow her the long way down the driveway. We crossed the street and headed down a small path to the church parking lot.

It was a fairly mild night. Helene had a light dusting of snow on the ground but at thirty-five degrees it was almost considered a warm front this far up north.

"I'm parked right here," Aimee said. She led me to her tan Lexus. I slipped into the passenger seat. Aimee turned the key to start her radio, then punched in 107.2 FM. "Joy to the World" was just ending. A moment later, a Mariah Carey

Christmas tune came on. I watched in awe as the LED elves in Nick's front yard came to life, dancing in time to the music. Colors bounced everywhere. The giant tree lit up, its star flashing to the tempo.

"This is incredible," I said.

"He's poured just about every penny he earns into this. Every year he adds something new. Those singing elves were last year's purchase. This year he was planning to have more reindeer up on the roof."

Sure enough, a red sleigh made of lights turned on. Nick even had a chimney up there constructed entirely of red and silver light bulbs.

I watched in amazement through three songs. During each one, different characters blazed to life and kept time with the music.

"That little Christmas cat is my favorite," Aimee laughed. Sure enough, on the downbeat of one of the songs, a little golden cat with a green yarn ball lit up in the far corner of the yard. All the way down the row, I saw parents and little kids in their cars, laughing and dancing while Nick's Christmas light show played.

"He has it set to play twenty different songs. About an hour's worth, then it starts up all over again. Most people stay for at least one cycle. And they'll come night after night, even though it's the same thing."

"It's wonderful. But the neighbors don't mind?"

"We didn't think they did. Then this zoning thing came up. Steve Anspaugh swore up and down he couldn't tell Nick who complained. It's just ... well, first ... since this is a county road, one of the county commissioners was concerned about it being a traffic hazard. It's gotten so big. Sometimes there will be a hundred cars out here."

"And he doesn't take money for this?"

"People try to make donations but Nick won't ever take it. It just makes him happy to make other people happy."

Someone tapped on Aimee's window. A young woman wrapped in a pink shawl peered in and smiled.

"Oh ... that's Dharma. I wanted you to meet her. Come on."

I got out of the car. The young woman smiled wide and extended her hand. She was pretty. Blonde hair pulled into a neat ponytail. Deep, appealing dimples in her cheeks.

"It's getting cold out here. Come on inside for some hot cocoa."

"Cass," Aimee said. "This is Dharma Till. She's Reverend Till's wife. This is their church."

"Oh," I said, shaking her hand. "I'm so glad to meet you. I was actually hoping to get a chance to talk to you."

I followed Aimee and Dharma into the narthex of the small church. Dharma led us past the double doors leading to the nave and took us to a small office down the hall. It was quaint, cozy with a red plush couch, an oak desk with two matching red chairs in front of it. Dharma went to the desk. She took two paper cups from a credenza behind it and poured steaming hot cocoa from a coffee carafe beside them. She handed me one.

"Thank you."

"Rich will be down here in a minute. He's just locking up."

"Reverend Till and Dharma have been a lifesaver," Aimee said, sipping her hot cocoa. "They organized a fundraiser to help pay for Nick's first lawyer."

"And we'll keep on doing it," Dharma said. "I know you don't work for free, Ms. Leary. And I know you probably didn't think you'd be spending your holidays here with us in Helene. But we're so happy you are."

"Well ... thank you. I just hope I can help."

"You already are," Aimee said. "Nick's in the best spirits I've seen him in since this whole thing started."

"Anything you need. Anything at all," Dharma said. "I know there are some people in this town who have already written poor Nick off. We're not among them. And there are a lot more like us than there are of the naysayers. You remember that, Aimee. We're all pulling for you and your whole family."

Aimee dabbed at a tear.

"There you are," a male voice came from behind me. I turned. A tall, lanky man with thick, wavy brown hair and bushy eyebrows walked in. He went to Dharma's side and laid a kiss on her cheek.

"Reverend Till, I presume," I said, rising from my chair.

He shook my hand with a firm, but not painful grip.

"Cass Leary," Aimee said. "I was just telling her how much of a godsend you and Dharma have been to our family."

"We've done so little," Rich Till said. "But we're praying. It's just so disheartening. A man who has brought such joy to everyone. It breaks my heart. Ms. Leary, do you think you can help our Nick?"

"I'm going to do my best."

"Her best is phenomenal!" Dharma gushed. "I've been reading about you. And I talked to Louise Malone, she's Judge Homer's stenographer. She said even the judge is impressed with your winning record. And he's not easily impressed with much."

"I kind of figured that out in his courtroom the other day," I said.

"Well, anything we can do to help," Reverend Till said.

"There is one thing I'd like to ask you about. Do you have any security cameras on the property? Something that might have picked up Nick's comings and goings on the night Mr. Anspaugh was attacked?"

Dharma's face fell. "I told Rich a thousand times. The year before we moved into the property, I heard someone stole money out of the collection box."

"This church has changed hands a few times," Aimee said.

"Aimee was our realtor too," Dharma added.

"The last ministry left before the pandemic. The church stood vacant for almost two years before Dharma and Reverend Till came in."

"It's been tough to build up our numbers," Reverend Till said. "People got out of the habit of worshiping in person. Everyone wants convenience. But we've grown each year. We have a core group of devoted parishioners. I wouldn't trade them for anything."

"We're inclusive here," Dharma said. "All are welcome. Do not be afraid, little flock, for the Lord has been pleased to give you the kingdom. Luke 12:32. His way of saying size doesn't matter, you know."

"Of course," I said. They hadn't even come close to answering my initial question. "But cameras?"

"No," Reverend Till said. "Dharma's been on me to install them but I don't want the people who come here thinking they're being judged by anyone but our Lord and Savior. If they are desperate enough to steal what few dollars we take in collections, well, then they're welcome to it."

"That's noble of you," I said. "Though I'm afraid anyone who would steal those few dollars probably isn't going to use them for good."

Reverend Till shrugged. "Again, it's not my place to judge."

"But it is our place," Dharma interjected. "That's why we were so happy when Aimee said you'd be coming out tonight. She said you've been staying downtown at the motel. You can't possibly be comfortable there."

"It's not so bad," I answered.

"Well, we want to invite you to stay here. There's a small guest house on the north end of our property. You might have passed it on your way in. It was a rectory long ago when the diocese owned this property. It's modest. But I've made some updates. It's one bedroom, a small study, a kitchenette, and a sitting room. You could spread out more. You know, for your trial preparation."

"That's ... wow. That's very generous." It was my instinct to say no. I didn't want to put these people out. But it occurred to me having ready access to Nick's house wouldn't be the worst thing. And Dharma had hit on something. It was cramped in Room 17.

"We have it hooked up to high-speed internet and Wi-Fi," Dharma said. "Please say you'll stay. It would do my heart good to help in some small way."

"It's not a small way," I said. "It's huge. Thank you."

"Free of charge, of course," Reverend Till added.

"I couldn't ..."

"It's not charity," Dharma interjected. "Don't think of it that way. We'd be doing it for Nick as much as for you. And I told you, anything you need. We haven't been here long, but I know everyone in town. I could help you prepare, you know ... for the witnesses Mr. Braunlin plans to call."

"But you might be one of them," I said. "I've seen Mr. Braunlin's witness list. Because of your proximity to Nick's house, I imagine."

"Well, I didn't see anything. I went to bed early that night. I'd just gotten over COVID."

"Please," Reverend Till said. "Let my wife help you. It'll bring her joy and ease her mind. Nick Whittaker was one of us."

"He was a member of your congregation?"

"He was," Till answered. "The Anspaughs too. At least for a little while. And Nick was a tireless volunteer. Nick took care of the grounds during the summer. Mowing, edging, weeding. And he's helped me more times than I can count moving things around in here. He helped Dharma with her renovations to the guest house you'll be staying in. You will be staying with us, won't you?"

Aimee and Dharma gave me an expectant look. I couldn't think of a good reason to say no, and realized I didn't want one.

"I'll be staying."

Dharma hugged her husband. He kissed the top of her head. Something made me turn and face the window. From there, I had a clear view of Nick Whittaker's Christmas light show.

"This would be the top of the hour finale," Aimee whispered. Sure enough, "Jolly Old Saint Nicholas" blared through the speakers of the cars parked closest to us. The chimney on Nick's house lit up along with the tree. Rudolph made his LED appearance, his red nose blinking.

"He'd come out the front door now," Aimee said. As soon as she said it, a spotlight shone on the door. The door itself was gift-wrapped in red with a shiny gold bow. But Nick Whittaker didn't come out. I found myself wondering if he ever would again.

Chapter 7

"You're where again?"

Eric Wray's deep voice flooded through and warmed me like good whisky.

"I'm still up north in Helene."

"Yeah. I didn't believe her when Jeanie told me. What the hell are you doing, Cass?"

"Trying to save Christmas?"

"Very funny."

"Well, seriously. This guy? Nick Whittaker? He means a lot to people around here. And my gut is telling me he's innocent. And I think he got royally screwed over by his last lawyer and nobody's willing to dive into that."

Eric grumbled, but didn't argue with me. He knew well enough not to once I'd made my mind up.

"So what do you need?"

There went that warm honey feeling again. I smiled. "I love you," I said.

"I love you too. But are you sure you're okay?"

I knew what he was asking. My coming to Helene at all had been fraught as far as he was concerned. But I was selling my last link to Killian Thorne, the man who had stood between us for far too long.

"I'm okay. And I think I've got this under control."

Eric's soft laughter gave me goosebumps. I found myself wishing he were here. I could handle all of this, but it would have been nice to have a partner in this just the same.

"So what's your theory? That surveillance footage was pretty damning."

"Jeanie sent it to you?"

"And I've checked out some of the news articles about it. Are you sure you can get a fair trial in that county?"

"No. But I'm stuck. Whittaker's previous lawyer already tried a change of venue motion and got shot down. Even so, there's reasonable doubt. All that tape shows is someone dressed up as Santa following Steve Anspaugh into the woods."

"And coming back out with the tire iron used to beat him within an inch of his life that was then found in your client's possession. How are you getting reasonable doubt from that?"

"It could have been planted. I'm gonna get the lead detective to admit they couldn't make a positive ID from that video footage. It's too grainy. Anybody could have been wearing that costume."

"You're gonna need more."

"I know."

"You need to figure out who else might have had a motive to kill Anspaugh. Are you making any headway with that?"

"For the most part, people around here are reluctant to talk to me. Hardly anyone on the prosecution's witness list will return my calls. I've got some notes from Tom Gale, Whittaker's last lawyer. A few of them talked to him but nobody saw anything after Anspaugh and Nick Whittaker left that party. It was well known in town that Anspaugh held the keys to a big part of Whittaker's identity."

"That light show?"

"It's impressive. It's like art, Eric. Whittaker's a talented guy. And he found his niche here. It kills me that he stands to lose it all. I just can't stand by and let him get locked up for this for the rest of his life."

"So again, I ask. What do you need? How can I help?"

"I'm not sure yet. I said most of the people on the prosecution's witness list don't want to talk to me. I do have a meeting with someone who worked with Anspaugh and who was also at the Christmas in July party that night."

"If you can find someone who had an ax to grind against the guy. Jeanie said you said he was pretty anti-development. That means there has to be someone out there who found themselves on the wrong side of his zoning board rulings. Let me see if I can stir anything up in that regard."

"That would be fantastic. Thank you."

"Though it seems pretty extreme to bash the guy's head in for that. Especially if he already ruled against them. And it's so ... I don't know ..."

"Passionate," I finished for him.

"Yeah. It's the kind of thing I'd see more often in a romantic entanglement. Or something involving a lot of money."

"Right."

"Was this guy married?"

"He was. Add his wife to the list of people who are refusing my calls. Word is she's pretty much sat vigil at his hospital bed for the last five months."

"Well let me do some checking on that as well. See if there are any criminal record skeletons buried in the Anspaugh closet."

"You won't find any. The Anspaughs are a founding family here. There's a street named after them, I'm told. This is a tiny town, Eric. Everyone knows everyone."

"Well, in my experience, not everyone knows everything. Everybody has secrets, even in small towns."

He grew silent. Eric himself harbored a pretty big skeleton in his own past. One I would take with me to my grave.

"I miss you," I said. "How are things in Raleigh?"

"Calm for the most part. My sister's kids have grown like weeds. My mom's hell-bent on having me clean out her attic while I'm here. And my dad? Well, he's having issues walking that he's trying to cover up. Mom wants me to bully him into seeing the doctor again. He's got an appointment next week."

"You'll take him? He'll let you take him?"

"I'm not gonna give him a choice."

"You're a good son, Detective Wray."

"I'll be home the day after Christmas. We'll plan something special, just the two of us. How does that sound?"

"Like heaven. We'll miss you though. Vangie's going all out this year. Insists on cooking everything herself."

"Let her. She's good at it."

"You don't like my cooking?"

Eric laughed. I was good at meatloaf and that was about it. Not a very Christmassy dish.

"I'll see what I can run down on Anspaugh or his family. And I'll check into the recent zoning requests for Helene Township."

"Again, I say, I love you."

"Yeah, yeah. Take care of yourself, kid. And drive safely heading back. The weather's gonna take a turn later in the week. What kind of rental did they put you in? I wish you would have waited to head up there after they finished the warranty work on your Jeep. It's got snow tires on it."

"Stop worrying," I said.

"Never."

"I'll call you tomorrow."

I clicked off, still smiling.

I was still in my cramped Room 17 but had packed all my trial prep files into the trunk of my car. Dharma Till was letting me use a spare office at the church to meet with Mildred Rapp, a long-time secretary for the Township Zoning Board. I had exactly fifteen minutes to get over there and wait for her.

Chapter 8

"SHE'S EARLY," Dharma Till whispered as she opened the side door of the church. "I'm sorry. I've got her set up down the hall."

"I appreciate it," I said. Dharma had her hair piled high today and wore a fetching, floral print dress. A pattern I could never pull off.

"Can I get you coffee? Tea? A soft drink? I already brought Mildred her hot water with lemon."

"I'm fine. And really, you've gone to so much trouble for me already. Please don't feel you have to wait on me."

Reverend Till came out of the vestibule. He gave his wife a stern look, then instantly brightened when he saw me.

"Ms. Leary. I hope you're settled in all right. If you need any help moving your things, just poke your head into my office."

"Thank you. Both of you."

Dharma held her hand out, gesturing toward the open doorway down the hall. I could just see a pair of chunky heels bobbing attached to a leg in sheer panty hose. Mildred Rapp, I presumed.

"Millie," Dharma said. "This is Cass Leary. She's the lawyer I was telling you about. She's gonna help Nick."

Mildred tried to get up but I could see it was going to take her more effort than was necessary.

"Please. Sit. Thank you for coming. I know it's your lunch hour."

"Oh!" Dharma said. "You've gotta let me bring you something. I was just getting ready to make sandwiches for Richard and me. Nothing fancy. Do you like tuna fish?"

Mildred waved Dharma off. "No, thank you, honey. You just enjoy your lunchtime with Reverend Till. He does so much for everyone else. So do you. Won't hurt me to skip a meal every now and again."

Dharma kept her bright smile in place and stayed in the doorway even after I'd taken a seat in the chair opposite Mildred Rapp. She stood there for a full minute before the looks both I and Mildred gave her sank in.

"Oh goodness! Here I am being a nosey Nellie. I'll leave you some privacy." With that, she turned on her heel and shut the door behind her.

"Sorry," Mildred said. She was maybe Jeanie's age, in her early seventies. She had tight dark curls and thinning patches of hair. She wore purple, cat-eye glasses with a jeweled chain that rattled when she talked.

"I really do appreciate you making time for me. I'll admit. It hasn't been easy getting people to talk to me about what happened."

"You're new," she said. "Helene is a pretty tight-knit community. We're welcoming. I hope you've seen that. But this whole affair has been just awful for everyone. I mean Mr. Anspaugh and Trudy especially. Have you met Trudy? Mr. Anspaugh's wife?"

"No. She ... uh ... she's one of the people I've had difficulty getting to talk to me."

"That poor woman's been through hell. Steve is her world. They never had any kids. We're so worried about her. Afraid she's going to stress herself into a stroke or a heart attack."

"I'm sure. I can't even imagine."

"So what is it you think I can help you with, honey? I gotta be honest. I wasn't sure this was a good idea for me either. But Reverend Till, he told me there's no harm in the truth. And people are still innocent until proven guilty around here."

"Of course. I'm grateful. I won't waste your time. Let's get right to it. How long have you known Steven and Trudy Anspaugh?"

"Well, Steve's been on the zoning board for almost ten years. His father, Garrett, held the seat before him. Oh, I'd say twenty-five years. I've been in the front office at the township since before he was elected. It'll be forty-one years in March. Everybody asks me when I'm going to retire. Not until the day I die, I say."

"That's amazing. So I guess that means you've seen everything, huh?"

"In this town? You betcha."

"Township Hall is right next to the library. You share a parking lot, is that right?"

"We do indeed. They repaved it last year. About time on that."

"The zoning commission, tax assessor, township supervisor, you're all housed in the same office?"

"Yes, ma'am. Parks commission too."

"I have to ask you. Are you aware of any enemies Mr. Anspaugh might have had?"

"Oh, the cops asked me that too. Detective Haney went to school with my son, Jordy. Nice boy. Good family."

"What did you tell him? Detective Haney." Haney was the lead detective on this case. I expected the prosecutor to put him on the stand first.

"Steve was a good guy. Sorry. He is a good man. He's abrupt. Direct, you know? He can come off as sort of a curmudgeon. But his heart's in the right place. And he loves this town. Everything he's done he's done to protect it."

"But he had to have made a few enemies along the way. People who wanted to develop or make changes to their property that he wouldn't allow?"

"Like Nick Whittaker," she said.

"Surely Nick wasn't the only person who'd ever faced denial of a variance they wanted, was he?"

"Oh no. Not at all."

"Was there anyone you can think of who might have gotten particularly upset? Were there any commercial developments held up by the zoning board?"

"From time to time. Amos Barnett's been trying to get that acreage off Mallard Road zoned for multi-family housing for years. I'll tell you what, Steve was never going to let that happen. Amos is nothing more than a slum lord and Steve told him so."

I wrote down the name.

"Did Mr. Barnett ever threaten Mr. Anspaugh?"

"They've had words over the years. But it's been years. Not recent."

"How much land are we talking about?"

"It's out on Mallard Road. If you take Dover as east as it'll go, you'll see the signs. Mr. Barnett can't sell it now. A sixty acres and it's too flat to hunt. I don't know why he doesn't farm it out. He's stubborn, that's why."

"Do you know how I can get a hold of Mr. Barnett?"

"He lives out there," she said. "Just drive right up. He's got for sale signs with his phone number on them. It won't do you any good though. Amos wasn't at the library party. He never comes to any of the town functions."

"Well, I appreciate the information, just the same. Do you think Mr. Anspaugh was going to vote against Nick's variance?"

"He was between a rock and a hard place on that. The master zoning plan is very clear. Nick was in violation when he put up that light show. And it is a traffic hazard. For years, the township just looked the other way. But if Mr. Anspaugh had ultimately denied that variance, it would have been in keeping with the letter of the law."

"The zoning board is within its purview to grant a variance though. That's within the letter of the law too."

"Oh, sure. And if he had ruled against Nick, a lot of people would have been pretty upset. Including me. I take my grandkids out to see that light show every year. Several times a year."

"So you really don't know which way Anspaugh was leaning?"

"No. Steve kept all that pretty close to the vest. But ... if I had to guess, I'd say he was going to feel like he had no choice but to deny the variance."

"The board hasn't put it to a vote since he was hospitalized though. They could have. I mean, the business of local government has to keep moving, doesn't it?"

"Nobody has had the heart to do anything about it. People are just sick about what's happened. They're in denial. They're waiting to see what happens with Nick's trial. Then I suppose after the holidays."

"They're figuring if Nick gets convicted, the light show will become a moot point."

"I should say so."

"What about Steve and Trudy? Do they have a good marriage? I know you said Steve is Trudy's world. Is that mutual?"

"Are you trying to stir something up? Because I'll tell you what, Missy, I don't stand for town gossip."

"And I'm not trying to stir any of it. I'm just trying to get the lay of the land. You understand Nick Whittaker is on trial for his freedom. For the rest of his life. It's my job to dig into this."

"Steve Anspaugh didn't deserve to be beaten."

I'd lost her. Mildred Rapp folded her arms across her chest and scowled at me.

"Of course not. Nobody deserves that. I want justice for him as much as anyone. I'm just trying to understand what might have been going on in his life in those last few months before he was attacked."

"Sure," she said. "Not everyone liked Steve. That comes with the territory when you're an elected official. But you won't find anyone who didn't think Steve was fair. Even if they didn't agree with him. As far as he and Trudy, I never saw anything untoward. She's been a good wife to him."

I bit my tongue past the retort I wanted to make. That didn't mean Steve had been a good husband to Trudy. But based on her demeanor, I didn't think the comment would go over well.

"But he got along with everyone?"

"I didn't say that. Steve was a stickler for the rules. Somebody has to be around here."

"Of course. Mildred, you told the police that you were at the library party the night of the attack. You told them you saw Nick and Steve Anspaugh having an argument. Can you tell me about that? What did you see? What did you hear?"

"I feel bad for Nick. Truly. I do. Everyone knows how much it means to him to be Santa for everyone. It's like his true calling. Oh, his parents would have been so proud about how things turned out for him. I mean ... until now. He's special, that Nick. A real loner, but a nice boy. At least I always thought so."

"Mrs. Rapp, the night of the library party though ..."

"Oh ... yes. I was getting to that. See, Nick doesn't like confrontation. He's a people pleaser. But he was so worried about what the zoning board was going to do. I don't even think he was planning on getting into it with Steve that night. But they just kept bumping into each other. And it was like this big elephant in the room. I'm sure Nick was wondering if this was going to be the last time he was allowed to run the light show. Heck, we were all wondering that. Anyway, I saw Nick and Steve in the hallway near the men's room. Nick was so upset. Saying 'You can't take this away from me. You just can't!' Steve was trying to calm him down. But he told Nick it wasn't the time and place to be having this conversation. And he sure didn't like that Nick was bringing it up with him one-on-one like that. Steve was always worried about the appearance of impropriety, you know? He's as straight-laced as they come."

"Did he threaten Steve? Did you hear anything like that?"

Mildred shrugged. "Well, it was pretty aggressive. Getting in Steve's personal space. You know, jabbing his finger in Steve's chest. He pushed him back."

I looked through my notes. "It says in the police report that you told Detective Haney it was Anspaugh who jabbed his finger in Nick's chest?"

"Did I? I don't remember that. Well, it was heated. That's all I'm saying."

"What did you do?"

"I minded my own business. That's what I did. They broke it up. Nick and Steve went their separate ways. At least, I thought they did. That's the last time I saw Steve."

"What about Nick? When's the last time you saw him?"

"You think I'm lying about what I saw?"

"Not at all. I'm just trying to get a sense of the timeline. Where everyone was and when."

"I don't know. I just don't know."

"You didn't see when Steve left the building?"

"No, ma'am."

"And you didn't see Nick again?"

"No, ma'am. I was trying to mind my own business. It wasn't until about an hour later before hell broke loose. Trudy came running into the library screaming."

"She's the one who found her husband."

"Can you imagine? See, here's the only big secret I knew about Steve Anspaugh. He was a smoker. He hid it from Trudy. But that night, I betcha he went out to have a cigarette. She went looking for him. Found him out there lying face down in the grass. Just awful. Never mind Steve. I just don't think Trudy is going to survive this."

"I really am sorry. I'm from a small town too, Mrs. Rapp. I understand how close everyone is, even if they're not technically friends."

"I'm sorry I can't be more helpful. We don't hate Nick. You need to know that. But we think he's a troubled soul. And faced with what he thought was the loss of his life's purpose? Well? I suppose anyone in that situation might feel backed into a corner."

This was not going as well as I hoped. Sympathetic or not, Mildred Rapp had clearly made her mind up about Nick Whittaker. I just had to hope we could find a jury of his peers that hadn't done the same exact thing.

And time was running out. In two days, the prosecution would deliver its opening statement.

Chapter 9

"IT STARTS HERE," Aimee said. She'd driven me to the very eastern edge of the township. A beautiful spot. Quite honestly, every inch of Helene had its own beauty. Rolling hills. The stunning expanse of Lake Michigan. Here, the woods opened up to flatlands. Aimee angled her car on the side of the road near a footbridge over a creek running north to south.

I slipped on a pair of sunglasses. The morning sun reflected off the packed snow, nearly blinding me. The wintry scene was marred only by two giant plywood signs with red spray-painted lettering. "For Sale. 60 Acres. Best offer."

"He's been trying to unload this parcel for I think three years now. I had a couple of offers for him, but he turned it all down. Thinks he's going to get a million for it."

"Is it buildable?" I asked.

"Sure," she said. "The trouble is, the north third of it is designated wetlands so that's protected. But there's nothing stopping Barnett from selling off some of these parcels near the road. He's been difficult to work with. Refuses to split any of this off."

I had my boots on. So did Aimee. We crossed the footbridge. On this particular strip of land, you could see clear out to the bay. Beyond it, I saw a small island. From this distance, smoke could be seen wafting over the trees.

"That's Tom Gale's place," she said. "He bought it for three million bucks and that was twenty years ago. It's worth a lot more now."

"How does he get back to the mainland?"

"During the winter? He doesn't much. He's got a snowmobile but I haven't seen him around town in weeks. To be honest, if I couldn't see the chimney smoke, I'd start wondering if he was okay. In the summer, he's got a boat slip at Lochlan Peak."

"Tell me about Amos Barnett, the guy who owns these sixty acres."

"He's a schemer. Always has some get-rich-quick plan or another. He's never gotten rich, but he keeps his head above water. He inherited part of this land from his father. Twenty acres of it anyway. He mortgaged his existing home for the down payment on the rest of it."

"Mildred Rapp said his plan was to build a modular home community here?"

"Yep. He should have cleared that with the township first. It got ugly for a little while after he was denied."

"How long ago was that?"

"Maybe four years."

"Hmm. That's a pretty long cooling-off period. Do you know whether Tom Gale talked to him? I know the cops didn't. That's one of many concerns I have about how this investigation was handled."

"I don't know about Tom. He wouldn't really talk to me. Then he stopped talking to everyone."

"It's a problem," I said. "A big one. I know you said he's being protected. I saw that for myself in Judge Homer's courtroom. I just didn't see anything in Gale's notes about Barnett. That's odd to me. It's the first question I asked. Who else might have a motive to do harm or seek revenge on Steve Anspaugh."

A beat-up pickup truck pulled in right behind Aimee's Lexus.

"Speak of the devil," she said. "Hey, Amos!" Aimee lifted her hand in a wave. Then under her breath to me, "Crap. He's probably got cameras out here somewhere. I was hoping we could avoid a confrontation."

"It's okay," I said. "It'll save me some time. I wanted to talk to him."

There were two people in the cab of the truck.

The driver got out. He was maybe fifty, wearing a hunter's orange knit cap and Carhart overalls. He had a two-day-old scruff on his face along with a scowl.

"I didn't get a call you were planning to show the place, Aimee," the man said.

"Cass," Aimee said. "This is Amos Barnett. Is that A.J. in the truck? Hey, there, A.J.!"

I lifted my hand to wave. As I walked closer, I could see A.J. was just a teenager. He slouched in his seat, his scowl rivaling that of who I assumed was his dad.

"Mr. Barnett?" I said, extending a hand to him. "I'm Cass Leary. I'm glad we ran into you. Do you have a minute?"

"It's all sixty acres. Did Aimee tell you that?"

"Cass isn't a potential buyer, Amos. She's here representing Nick."

"Yeah?" Amos said. "Then I suppose you can get the hell out of here."

"Wait," I said. "Mr. Barnett, please. I've just got a question for you."

"Forget it. I know your type. Sleazy defense lawyers. No, thanks. I've got no time for you and you're both trespassing."

Amos turned and trudged back to his truck. I followed him.

"Mr. Barnett, I just want to ask you. Did Detective Haney talk to you after Steve Anspaugh's attack? Were you ever interviewed by the police?"

He kept walking. He opened the driver's side door and reached into the back seat.

"My dad's got nothing to say to you," A.J. shouted.

Amos turned around. He was holding a shotgun in his hand.

"Whoa," I said. "Just calm down. I'm just trying to get a complete picture of what happened."

"By coming out here?" Amos shouted. "I know your game. You think because me and Steve had our differences you can try to pin something on me. I'll make this real simple. Steve Anspaugh is a power hungry pain in my ass. A snob. A drain on taxpayer money. Do I think he deserved what happened to him? You know? Maybe he did. Who knows? But if you think you can come out here stirring up trouble. Dragging me into it. Lady, you have no idea who you're dealing with. Unless you'd like to find out the hard way, I suggest you get back into that piece of crap car Aimee's driving and disappear."

"I'm only trying to figure out how thorough Detective Haney's investigation was, that's all."

"Amos, you knock it off!" Aimee shouted. "Get back in your truck and go home. A.J. doesn't need to be part of this either. You should be ashamed of yourself."

"This is my property," Amos said. "I've got a right to be here. You don't. Next time, you don't set foot on this land without calling me for permission. And not even then unless you've got a legitimate buyer interested."

"You lost a lot of money on this property," I said. "That had to have been pretty frustrating. I've heard that Steve was anti-development. Is there anybody else you can think of that might have run afoul of Steve Anspaugh's zoning board rulings?"

"All that crap is public record," he said. "Don't stand there lying to me. I know why you're here. Time for you to crawl back under whatever rock you came from."

"Dad, let's go," A.J. shouted. The kid was miserable. Though it was hard to tell completely from his position inside the truck, the kid looked huge. He had a round, doughy face and hands roughly the size of dinner plates. His father was tall as well, but with a trim build except for his barrel chest. That said, he was

75

the right size. I tried to imagine him wearing the Santa costume I'd seen in the library surveillance video.

"Cass," Aimee said. "This was a bad idea. Let's just go. Amos is clearly not capable of having a rational conversation."

"Nick's a nutcase, Aimee. You're wasting your time and your money on him. And I meant what I said. I see you out here again without my permission, I'll make you sorry."

"Are you threatening her?" I said.

"Cass, let's go."

Aimee was already halfway to the car. I didn't want to turn my back on this lunatic. The boy frowned at me from the passenger seat. But Amos finally climbed back into his truck. He revved his engine in a different kind of threat. Was he actually going to try running me over?

I went back to Aimee's car and climbed in. She wasted no time and jammed it in drive.

"Crazy bastard," she said.

"I don't understand why Mark Haney never interviewed him," I said. "Barnett has a well-known beef against Steve Anspaugh based on what you and everyone else has said."

"Because Haney made up his mind that night," Aimee answered. "And because Amos and Mark Haney are old hunting buddies."

My cross-examination of Detective Mark Haney could practically write itself at this point.

"I feel bad for that kid," I said. "A.J."

"Everyone feels bad for that kid. Though it's sad to say, A.J. is probably doomed to turn out just like his sour old man."

"Is there a Mrs. Barnett in the picture?"

"Sadie? No. She split years ago. Amos's drinking got to be too much for her. Though he's been sober for a few years. Sadie just couldn't take it anymore."

"But she left the boy?"

"Like I said, the whole town feels sorry for A.J. We've all tried to help in some way or another. Nick has a soft spot for him. When he was little, after Sadie left, Nick always made sure to have something special for A.J. when he'd show up for pictures with Santa. Some years I wondered if that was the only present A.J. got."

"That's really sweet."

"That's Nick. He's also got an uncanny ability to find the perfect gift for people."

Aimee turned, taking the road back into town.

"Has Amos ever gotten physical with anyone? Bar fights? Or with Sadie?"

Aimee shrugged. "I can't answer you about Sadie."

"Do you think somebody like Mark Haney might have protected him if he had?"

"I hope not. But I don't know. As far as bar fights? Probably. I know Amos has a DUI or two. Not recently though. Cass, do you think he could have done this?"

"Do you?"

"It just makes no sense. There's bad blood between Amos and Anspaugh. That's well known. But it's been years since that flared up. And why would he go to the trouble of dressing up like Nick to get revenge or whatever that was?"

My mind spun. "Could he have been jealous of Nick? I mean, if Amos was insecure or feeling guilty about not being able to afford Christmas presents for his own kid and Nick showed up with the perfect thing, maybe it triggered some kind of jealousy in Amos."

"I suppose so. I just don't know. How do we find out if Amos had an alibi the night Steve Anspaugh was attacked?"

"Those are good questions," I said. "And they're ones Detective Haney should have been asking."

Questions. I had many more of those than I had answers. I just hoped it would be enough to raise reasonable doubt for Nick Whittaker.

Chapter 10

Nick Whittaker broke out into a cold sweat beside me. He trembled in his seat. I tried to reassure him. Wanted to tell him everything was going to be all right. But as the twelve men and women who would decide his fate filed in and took their seats in the jury box, I had real concern Nick might fall over in a faint.

"Mr. Braunlin, are you ready to proceed?" Judge Homer said in a clear, strong voice. Today, Judge Homer wore what I'd been told was his trademark red bowtie. He wore the same one for every trial he'd presided over since the day of his investiture. There was talk the local history museum wanted it to put on display after this trial was over. His very last.

"I am, Your Honor."

Lucas Braunlin was a different kind of relic in Helene County. Another legacy citizen. I learned he was on a short list to take over Judge Homer's seat. His father had also been a Circuit Court Judge for Helene County, retiring a decade ago.

Lucas. Though he told me just before we walked into the courtroom that everyone called him Lucky.

Of course they did.

"Ladies and gentlemen of the jury," Lucky Braunlin started. "This is a hell of a job you've been asked to do. I realize that. The irony isn't lost on me. Here we are, just a few short days from Christmas, and you're being asked to decide whether Santa Claus committed a brutal attack on a defenseless man.

"He looks the part, doesn't he? For the last twenty years, Nick Whittaker has delighted the citizens of this town playing Saint Nick for school events, parades, even outside his own house. I know many of you have seen his Christmas light show. You've made it part of your holiday experience. Mine too.

"But here's the thing I need you to do. The thing the law demands that you do. You've gotta forget about what you think you see when you look at Nick Whittaker. Because that's his name. He's no saint. He's certainly not Santa Claus. What he is, is a violent loner. A pretender. He's played a role his whole life and now it's time to reveal his true identity."

Braunlin stood at the lectern, leaning on it with his left elbow. He was handsome. Well-coiffed auburn hair, a straight nose, and lean build. He was younger than me, just thirty-six, according to what I'd read online. He had a big, Catholic family. Five kids and his wife worked as a cashier down at Holly's Food Mart, though Dharma said she didn't need to. Lucky. Just like her husband.

"Over the next couple of days, that's my job. My promise to you," Braunlin continued. "I'm going to strip Nick Whittaker of his disguise. Show you what he did. What he's still capable of."

Beside me, Nick dropped his head. His beard nearly touched the table. I resisted the urge to put a comforting arm around him. He seemed almost child-like today. Behind me Aimee

Whittaker sat with two other Whittaker cousins. She promised Nick they wouldn't leave his side. I just prayed he'd draw strength from them.

"The evidence will show that on the evening of July 25th, faced with the destruction of what Nick has always believed was his identity, he chose violence. He saw Steven Anspaugh as a threat to his very existence and he took him out. You're going to be instructed about your burden of proof in this case. Reasonable doubt. Though I'm going to tell you, when you hear from Detective Mark Haney, when you see the physical evidence in this case, when you understand from witness testimony just how angry Nick Whittaker was with Steve Anspaugh, I can assure you, you'll have no doubt whatsoever that Nick Whittaker, and only Nick Whittaker committed this heinous act."

Nick shook his head. Softly, he whispered, "No, no, no."

"Shh," I said. "I warned you this would be hard to hear. Just stay with me."

"Steven Anspaugh will probably never wake up again. Never look into his wife's face. Never tell her he loves her. Never spend another Christmas at the hearth of his family home. All because he was doing his job. Fulfilling his solemn oath to the people of this town. He didn't deserve what happened to him. And what did happen to him? Well, Steven Anspaugh was beaten so badly ... his orbital bone smashed, his jaw broken, his skull fractured. His brain swelled so much that doctors had to drill a hole through his skull to relieve the pressure. It's a miracle he's still alive. But let me tell you, it's not a life that anyone would wish for. Hooked up to machines. Unable to talk. Unable to tell his wife or the rest of his family that he loves them. He lies in a hospital just a few miles from here in a coma. An eternal sleep. I wish there were some other charge we could bring against this man other than attempted murder. Because make no mistake, Nick Whittaker has taken a life even though Steven Anspaugh still draws breath. He has imprisoned this poor man inside his own body. We'll never know what Steven Anspaugh's experience in life is now. Can he hear? Does he know the state he's in? It's a horror few can imagine. And for what? Because of Christmas lights?"

Braunlin shook his head, acting as if he could no longer find the words. A tactic. Theatrics, maybe. Only he was right. No one could ever know what level of awareness Steven Anspaugh had now. I saw a shudder go through a few members of the jury. It was an effective opening statement, if not conventional. As if I hadn't already known it, I had my work cut out for me.

Behind the prosecution's table, Trudy Anspaugh quietly wept. She was a slight woman. Blonde hair sprayed into submission on top of her head. She wore silver dangling earrings that reflected the light from the windows behind the jury.

"Thank you," Lucky Braunlin said. "That's all I have to say to you for now."

Judge Homer gestured me forward. I gave Nick a tight-lipped smile and stepped up to the lectern.

"Good morning," I said. "My name is Cass Leary. I know I'm an unfamiliar face to you. New to this town. I've been welcomed to it though and I appreciate that."

I took a different strategy than Lucky Braunlin. While he stayed at the lectern, I liked to move. I stood in front of the jury box and made eye contact with each and every juror at one point or another during my statement.

"I'm glad Mr. Braunlin brought up the issue of identity. He says he wants to dispel the myth of who Nick Whittaker really is. Peel off a mask, so to speak. Though I do find it interesting that he didn't mention some of the things this case hinges on. It will hinge on what you can see with your very own eyes. Mr. Braunlin is going to have to ask you to make assumptions about that. What you're seeing. Well, I'm going to ask you to keep your eyes open. Your minds too. Just because something looks a certain way, doesn't mean it is a certain way.

"The evidence Mr. Braunlin wants to show you may look bad for Nick Whittaker. But only if you believe the story Mr. Braunlin has to sell you. Only if you take his word for what you're actually seeing. Remember that. Ask yourself this simple question with each piece of evidence the prosecution tries to introduce. Am I really seeing something, or am I being told what to see? Am I being told what to believe? If the answers to your questions are yes, if you have to believe Mr. Braunlin's story rather than what you can see with your own eyes, then the state will have failed to meet its burden of proof.

"Reasonable doubt. Mr. Braunlin is right. You'll be instructed by the judge on what that is. I believe that when this case is over, when it's your turn to deliver a verdict, you'll see that all you were given was a story. One that can only be true if you see things through Mr. Braunlin's eyes, not your own."

I paused. I walked back to the lectern and took my place behind it.

"Yes. Nick Whittaker has played a role for the people of this town. Devoted son. Tireless volunteer. Electrician. And yes, Santa Claus when he's asked to. It's something that brings him as much joy ... no ... more joy than even the people he performs for. He has lived among you, been one of you, for his entire life.

He is who he says he is. It's not a mask. It's not a lie. And he did not hurt Steven Anspaugh."

I folded my hands and rested them on the lectern. "I cannot imagine how difficult this has been on Steve Anspaugh's family. There's no denying the brutality of the attack on him. It's horrible. Unthinkable. He deserves justice. His family deserves justice. But Nick Whittaker didn't commit this crime. When all is said and done, all the state has is evidence that looks bad for Mr. Whittaker. And that is not enough. Not by a long shot. Nick Whittaker didn't commit this crime. When you look at the facts, and that is all you can look at, ladies and gentlemen, you will see reasonable doubt. You'll see the prosecution's case is full of holes wide enough to drive a truck through. And I'm confident that you'll return with a verdict of not guilty. Thank you."

I went back to my seat at the table. Nick looked calmer. He'd stopped sweating. Stopped shaking. He'd written a note on the legal pad in front of him.

"Thank you for believing in me."

I put my hand over it then gave him a thumbs up.

"Mr. Braunlin?" the judge said. "Are you ready to call your first witness?"

"Of course, Your Honor. The state calls Detective Mark Haney to the stand."

Nick took an audible breath. Deputy Detective Haney strode confidently through the gallery and climbed into the witness box, his silver badge shining under the harsh lights. He raised his right hand and swore to tell the truth.

Chapter 11

"How long have you been with the Helene County Sheriff's Department, Detective?"

Lucky Braunlin leaned against the lectern. He kept a smile fixed in place and looked at the jury, rather than his witness.

"Twenty-one years this past May," Detective Mark Haney said. A true ginger, Haney had forearms dotted with freckles and a red handlebar mustache. He wore a pair of reading glasses perched at the end of his nose.

"You gettin' ready to retire?" Braunlin asked.

"Oh, my wife would like that. She's been on me since I hit my twenty. But I like the work. I think I'll stick around until I hit at least twenty-five."

"How many detectives does the county have handling violent crimes?"

"Me, mainly. We've got Cynthia Schumacher handling property crimes. We've got Paul Dulaney dealing with the schools. But we're the three musketeers."

"How long have you been in your current position?"

"Sixteen years."

"Good man," Braunlin said. I was getting a little tired of the good old boy act, but it wasn't exactly objectionable.

"So how did you become associated with this terrible case, Detective?"

"I received a call from dispatch on the evening of July 25th. A little after ten p.m. The responding officer, Deputy John Short, was still on scene when I got there."

"Got where, Detective?"

"Oh, sure. Sorry. Let me start from the beginning. Anyway, dispatch told me Shorty ... er ... Deputy Short needed me out at the library. There'd been an incident in the parking lot. Suspected mugging is what I think Deputy Short said. I was already at home, you see. My shift normally ends at five. I texted my lieutenant, Daisy Gross, to make sure she'd approve the overtime. No trouble there. So, I put my suit back on and headed over to the library."

"What did you find when you got there?"

"The victim, Steven Anspaugh, had already been transported by ambulance to the county hospital with life-threatening injuries. Deputy Short arrived just a few minutes before I did. George and Mildred Rapp met us along with Emily Connor, the head librarian. I was aware there had been a Christmas in July party at the library that had just wrapped up. Most of the people had left. Emily, the Rapps, and a few onlookers were still there. Emily was pretty upset. She informed me that Trudy Anspaugh had gone out to the parking lot as the party started winding down to look for her husband. She found him lying face down about two feet off the hiking trail behind the library. He was unconscious and bleeding from wounds to his head. Emily heard Trudy calling for help and went running. Emily's the one who called 9-1-1."

"Did you see the victim at that time?" Braunlin asked.

"No, sir. As I said, Mr. Anspaugh had already been transported to the local hospital."

"What did you do next?"

"I interviewed the Rapps and Emily Connor. I asked for a list of every person who'd attended the party, but Emily didn't have one. It wasn't like you needed an invitation. There was no sign-in sheet. But the Rapps and Emily did their best to recall everybody they knew who'd been there. I gotta be honest, it was just about half the town. More. I'd say anybody who had kids under ten showed up that night to get their pictures with Santa, you know?"

"Sure. What'd you do next?"

"I asked the Rapps and Emily if they saw anything unusual. If they could tell me anything about Steve Anspaugh's movements that night. Who he talked to primarily. That sort of thing. Emily got pretty agitated at that point. I had a sense she knew something but was afraid to tell me. So I had her walk with me outside. Thought maybe if I got her away from the others she might be more willing to be forthright."

"Was she?"

"She said she'd seen Steve arguing with Nick Whittaker. She said it was disturbing because Nick was already fully suited up as Santa by then. Emily said she actually went up to Nick and told him whatever was going on between the two of them, that party wasn't the time or the place to get into it."

"Did she indicate how the defendant, Mr. Whittaker, responded to all of this?"

"She said—"

"Objection, Your Honor, this is hearsay. If Mrs. Connor is going to take the stand in her own right, she's more than capable of describing what she observed."

Braunlin didn't move a muscle. Detective Haney looked at the judge.

"I'll sustain that one. Detective, you're free to testify about what actions you took as a result of what you were told, but Ms. Leary's right. Mrs. Connor will be the best witness to describe her own observations."

"Sure," Haney said.

"What did you do after you spoke to Mrs. Connor?" Braunlin asked.

"Well, I knew they'd installed security cameras in the parking lot between Township Hall and the library. I figured it might be a long shot for them to have picked up anything, but Mr. Anspaugh was found off the trail. There's only one way to get there and that's through the parking lot. So, I asked Emily if she could show me that feed. Oh ... but I should add. Before I went back into Emily's office, I had a conversation with the Rapps. They too ... well, mostly Mildred. She'd seen Whittaker and Mr. Anspaugh having an argument of some kind just outside the men's room about two hours before the party broke up and Mr. Anspaugh was found."

"Okay. So what about this surveillance tape?"

"It's not a tape. It's all digital now. But I went in the office with Emily and had her play back the footage from the start of the party forward. I was able to see the comings and goings of just about everyone who attended the party so that was extremely helpful. I was able to eventually put together a pretty comprehensive list of everybody who was there that night."

"What else did you see?"

Haney let out a sigh. To his credit, he appeared pained by the testimony he was about to give.

"At the nine twenty-eight p.m. timestamp, Steve Anspaugh was seen leaving the library out the front door. There's no audio on the playback, but I personally know Steve. He came out and appeared to be arguing with someone. A moment later, someone came outside with him. It was Nick Whittaker."

Nick bristled beside me.

"Nick Whittaker," Braunlin slowly repeated. "Your Honor, at this time, I'd like to introduce State's Exhibit One."

It was clumsy of him. But we'd already stipulated to the entry of the raw footage. Emily Connor had provided an affidavit authenticating it.

"No objection," I said.

"Excellent," Braunlin said. He cued up the playback on the large monitor over Detective Haney's shoulder.

Braunlin had the tape start at the nine twenty-seven p.m. mark. The jury watched as Anspaugh emerged from the library. The seconds ticked as he wordlessly gestured toward someone still in the lobby. Then, the figure in the Santa suit emerged. A few members of the jury gasped. I'd warned Nick not to show any reaction to this. I told him to simply stare straight ahead.

I knew how torturous it was for him to watch the jury devour that footage. Each of them, likely jumping to an obvious conclusion. I'd told Nick it would be okay. My entire theory of the case hinged on convincing them not everything they saw was as it seemed.

Anspaugh backed up as the Santa figure advanced. Then the two of them walked out of frame and toward the hiking trails.

Braunlin let the tape play in its entirety. One minute went by. Two. Five. Then exactly twenty-two minutes and fourteen seconds after Anspaugh and the man in the Santa suit walked off, only one man returned.

His head was down, his hat pulled low. But Santa Claus strode back into frame carrying that black tire iron then disappeared out of frame in the opposite direction.

Braunlin stopped the playback.

"Detective, what did you think after viewing that tape?"

"Well, I wish I could say I was shocked. But after both the Rapps and Emily Connor said they'd witnessed an argument between the defendant and the victim, this just backed up their stories."

"I see. What did you do next?"

"I asked Emily when was the last time she saw Nick Whittaker. She couldn't remember precisely. I didn't think that much mattered so I left the rest of the canvassing to Deputy Short and headed over to the hospital to find out Anspaugh's condition and talk to his wife."

"Did you learn anything new?"

"Not really. I mean, other than the extent of Steve's injuries. At that point, the doctor wasn't optimistic he was gonna survive the night. He looked pretty bad. Barely human, actually."

With that, Braunlin introduced the photographs taken at the hospital the night Anspaugh was admitted. They were gruesome. His eye bulged out of its socket. His hair was matted down with blood. One side of his face was caved in from where he'd been struck.

"You ever seen anything like that?" Braunlin asked.

Haney had his head down, clearly shaken by having to review those photographs again.

"No, sir, not on somebody who was still hanging on to life. It's a miracle he didn't die. I'll tell you that."

"Did you learn anything that aided in your investigation at the hospital?"

"I asked to see Steve's clothing and personal effects."

"Why did you do that?"

"Well, I wanted to make sure this wasn't a mugging. I wanted to know whether anything of value had been taken from the victim."

"Was it?"

"Not that I could tell. Steve's wallet was still in his pants pocket. He had almost two hundred dollars cash in it. His phone. His credit cards. It was all still on him. He was also wearing his wedding ring and a gold chain around his neck. So I inferred that robbery wasn't a motive in this case."

"What did you do next?"

"I talked to Trudy briefly. Took her statement. She was able to tell me that it was just after ten when she went out looking for Steve. I didn't tell Trudy Anspaugh about the surveillance footage at the library. I saw no point in upsetting her and I knew I needed to talk to Nick anyway. I made sure Trudy had someone with her, then headed over to Nick's residence."

"What time was that?"

"It was a little after eleven that night. Actually, it was almost midnight. The lights were dark. I knew Nick was running his Christmas light show to coincide with the festivities we had going on in town."

"Was he home?"

"He was. He was pretty surprised to see me. I asked him to tell me his movements that night. He said he'd been at the library until nine thirty then came home so he could make his customary appearance out the front door at ten o'clock on the dot."

"What'd you do then?"

"I asked him about his beef with Steve Anspaugh."

"What did he say, if anything?"

"He claimed there was no beef. He denied having any argument with Steve that night or any other night. I told him there were witnesses who said otherwise. He stopped talking to me after that except to ask me if he was in some kind of trouble."

"What did you do then?"

"Well, I asked Nick if he wouldn't mind coming down to the sheriff's station with me to answer more questions. He got pretty agitated after that. Wanted to know if he was in trouble. Over and over he asked me that. Finally, I had to tell him yes. That he might be in trouble."

"Then what did you do?"

"Well, it's what he did. Nick said if he was in some kind of trouble, he didn't want to come with me unless he had a lawyer. And he asked me to recommend one to him. I said I couldn't do that but of course I was gonna respect his wishes. At that point, Nick changed his mind and said he'd come down to answer questions with me. So he got in my vehicle and I drove him down to the station."

"Then what happened?"

"Once we got to the station, I asked Nick if he could account for his whereabouts from nine thirty to nine fifty-two p.m. on the night of the 25th. He said he was at home, getting ready for the light show. He makes a kind of grand finale appearance during one of the Christmas songs he plays. I've seen it. It's pretty neat. Anyway, he was supposed to be out there at ten on the dot. That's what he said. I have to admit. I was hopeful. I figured it would be pretty easy to check that story."

"Why's that?"

"Well, there were probably thirty cars sitting outside his house that night waiting for him to come out. I happened to know that Daisy Gross's daughter was going to take her grandkids out there that night. So I called her."

"Lieutenant Gross?"

"I called her daughter, Lesley Jean. Anyway, Lesley confirmed that yes, she was out there watching the light show. But when I asked her if Nick made his appearance at ten, she said that he hadn't. That he was late coming out by almost a half an hour. She said a bunch of the people out there were pretty disappointed because their little kids were getting antsy. Then she remembered that the car next to her was recording it on a cell phone. I asked her if she knew who it was in that car. She said it was Russ Garfield. So he was my next call. He texted a copy of his cell phone video. Through it, I was able to confirm that Nick Whittaker wasn't out in front of his house until almost ten thirty that night."

"Did you ask Nick about that?"

"I did. He told me he had some problem with Rudolph that night and so he was running late. I asked him if anyone could confirm his story about Rudolph. Or if anyone might have seen when he arrived at home. He couldn't. He had no alibi. I told him that. He got pretty upset, as you can imagine. He said he didn't want to answer any more questions without having a lawyer with him."

"Of course," Braunlin said. "What did you do next?"

"Like I said, Nick said he wouldn't answer any more questions without a lawyer. He asked if he could make a phone call. We let him. He called his cousin, Aimee, and she told him the same thing, as far as I know. So we were at a bit of a stalemate. So while we were waiting for Nick to figure out if he was gonna get a lawyer, I wrote out a search warrant for his house. At that point, I'd seen the surveillance footage and had probable cause to believe Nick had committed this crime and I wanted to secure whatever evidence he might have back at his house. Namely the Santa costume he might have been wearing that night. The warrant came back pretty quick. Nick stayed in holding and I was back out at his house by five in the morning."

"Did you find anything incident to your search warrant?"

"Yes, sir. We collected three Santa suits out of Nick's closet. And when we searched around his house, we looked inside his garbage can. Found a tire iron right on top."

"What did you do?"

"We collected the evidence and I wrote out an arrest warrant. At that time, I formally arrested Nick Whittaker for the attack on Steve Anspaugh."

Braunlin introduced the tire iron and all three Santa costumes Nick owned.

"Detective, with regard to the tire iron, what did you do with it?"

"We contacted the Michigan State Police crime lab. They ran an analysis on the tire iron. It came back positive."

"What do you mean?"

"I mean there was indeed blood and DNA on it matching that of the victim, Steven Anspaugh. I concluded it was the weapon used to beat him."

"Is that the only physical evidence you recovered?"

"No, sir, I also sent the clothes Anspaugh was wearing to the lab. They were able to recover several fibers on his shirt that matched the threads to Mr. Whittaker's Santa costume as well as white synthetic fibers consistent with a wig."

Through all of it, Braunlin never let his gaze leave the jury. It was odd to me that he didn't look at Detective Haney. I wondered if the jury would pick up on that or if they'd care.

"Thank you, Detective, I have no more questions for now."

Judge Homer looked at the clock. "All right, Ms. Leary, you may cross-examine the witness."

Chapter 12

"Detective Haney," I said, stepping up to the lectern. "I want to make sure I'm clear on a few things."

"Yes, ma'am."

"You formed probable cause to arrest Mr. Whittaker on five things, if I understood your testimony. One, an identification you made from the videotape Emily Connor played you. Two, a tire iron found near Mr. Whittaker's residence with Mr. Anspaugh's blood on it. Three, clothing and wig fibers found on Mr. Anspaugh's person the night of the attack. Four, an alleged argument that took place between Mr. Anspaugh and Mr. Whittaker the night of the attack. And five, what you concluded was a lack of an alibi for Mr. Whittaker. Am I missing anything?"

"I'm not claiming there was a lack of an alibi. He had no alibi. Or, at the very least, the alibi he provided just didn't check out."

I tapped my pen against the side of the lectern. "I see. Well, I'd like to ask some follow-up questions about each of those five points."

"Of course, ma'am."

"With regard to the surveillance tape at the library on the night of July 25th. You yourself made the identification, isn't that right?"

"I recognized the suspect, yes."

"You recognized him. You mean the suit. You recognized the suit, isn't that right?"

"I'm sorry?"

"I mean, you're not claiming you could actually see the suspect's face in that video, are you?"

"Well, no. His back was turned. And the camera is actually mounted on a light pole about fifty yards from the back entrance."

"I'd like to replay a portion of that video for you now," I said, cuing up playback where the suspect's face appeared in profile, just before Anspaugh started walking out of view onto the hiking trails. I paused the playback.

"There," I said. "If you're just looking at the face of the suspect, do you recognize who it is?" I maximized the image. Doing so made the facial features even more blurry.

"I don't understand the question."

"You can't make out who that is by their facial features, isn't that right?"

"Not alone, no."

"And you tried to enhance the video, didn't you? To make it less blurry?"

"We used video enhancement techniques, yes."

"But isn't it true that with regard to the suspect in this video ... you weren't able to produce an image with any real clarity?"

"We couldn't make it clearer with regard to the face."

"So again, I say, it was the suit. You made the ID off the suit this person is wearing, isn't that right?"

"Well, that and the fact that about thirty people saw Mr. Whittaker and only Mr. Whittaker in that suit within minutes of this video capture."

"But nobody claims to have seen Mr. Whittaker actually walk out after Mr. Anspaugh, did they?"

"I'm sorry?"

I felt Detective Haney was being obtuse on purpose. I squared off to face him. "Emily Connor. Mr. and Mrs. Rapp, the other twenty party attendees you interviewed in your report. Not a single one told you they actually saw Nick Whittaker walk out the front door of that library, either after Mr. Anspaugh or at all."

"Um ... no. But they didn't need to. We've got it on video."

"All right. Let's move on. The second piece of evidence you used to form probable cause. The tire iron. Let's go back to the video. You can't see this suspect holding anything in his or her hands while walking out of the library entrance, can you?"

"No. Though it's hard to make out. And you can't really see the individual's right hand at all. But no, you can't specifically see a tire iron or anything else as they're walking out. But it's clearly there when they are emerging from the hiking trail alone."

"Okay. But again, the suspect's face isn't visible while he or she is walking back and out of frame. Their head is down."

I played that portion of the video again. The Santa figure with the tire iron walked with a distinct posture, his head down, his hat pulled low.

"No, he doesn't look up at the camera."

"He doesn't look up at the camera. In fact, he seems to be making a calculated effort not to face the camera, wouldn't you say?"

"Objection," Braunlin said. "Calls for speculation. Ms. Leary is trying to have the detective imagine a motivation for what the suspect is doing at that point in the tape."

"Sustained, Ms. Leary," Judge Homer said. "Let's stick to observable facts."

"Observable facts. Of course. Detective, what do you observe about the individual as he or she is passing directly in front of the camera mounted on that light pole?"

I rewound and replayed the portion of the tape. Again, we watched as the suspect emerged from the trail, then dropped his head as he came within view of the light pole.

"There," I said, stopping the tape. "What do you observe the suspect doing? He puts his head down there, doesn't he?"

"Yes."

"Hmm. Almost as if he knows the camera's there. And the suspect is carrying the tire iron in his right hand. The hand facing the camera, right?"

"Yes. It's in his right hand."

"About that tire iron, you located it in a trash bin on Mr. Whittaker's property, correct?"

"Correct. And just a few hours after the assault. The blood on it was still wet."

"I see. The trash can was kept outside the garage, wasn't it?"

"It was a blue can just outside the service door to Mr. Whittaker's garage, yes."

"The can wasn't locked, was it?"

"No, ma'am."

"How far down into the trash bin did you find the tire iron?"

"What do you mean?"

"Well, I mean ... from the evidence photos you took, there doesn't appear to be any other trash on top of it. Was there?"

"Um ... no, ma'am. It was right on top."

"Right on top. Thank you. Now, you've indicated the tire iron was still wet with blood."

"Mr. Anspaugh's blood, yes."

"There was a significant amount of blood found on that hiking trail, wasn't there? You found it on the ground. Splattered on the trunk of the tree closest to where Mr. Anspaugh was found. And of course, Mr. Anspaugh himself was bleeding profusely. In the hospital photographs introduced, Mr. Anspaugh is covered in blood, is he not?"

"That's true. Yes, ma'am."

"Incident to your search warrant, you found and secured three Santa suits from Mr. Whittaker's bedroom closet, isn't that right?"

"That's right."

"But you didn't find a single drop of blood on any of those suits, did you? Not belonging to Mr. Anspaugh and not belonging to Mr. Whittaker, correct?"

"There was no blood on Mr. Whittaker's Santa suits. That's correct."

"You confiscated three pairs of white gloves along with those suits, correct?"

"Yes."

"And we can clearly see the suspect wearing white gloves in the surveillance tape, correct?"

"Yes, ma'am."

"But none of the gloves you confiscated from Mr. Whittaker had blood on them, did they?"

"No, ma'am."

"And you say you found the tire iron in the trash, but no gloves or any other items of clothing or anything else with blood on it, correct?"

"Well, no, not the items you listed, no. There was a little bit of blood on a paper bag directly beneath the tire iron. It was laying on top of it."

"Got it. So no blood on Mr. Whittaker's suits. No blood on the gloves you found. Just on the tire iron and Mr. Anspaugh himself as well as out at the crime scene."

"That's correct."

"And what was Mr. Whittaker wearing when you went to his home that night?"

"He was still wearing the pants and boots from a Santa costume. He had a white tee shirt and red suspenders on. He had a jacket hung up on a hook by the front door."

"You took him to the police station in that clothing, correct?"

"Yes, ma'am."

"And later, after he was arrested and booked, you confiscated that costume, the one he was wearing."

"Yes, ma'am."

"And there was no blood on it, right?"

"No blood."

"All right. You said you found synthetic white fibers on Mr. Anspaugh's clothing. Later you determined that it came from a wig, isn't that right? A white wig?"

"Yes, ma'am."

"Detective, you personally know Nick Whittaker, don't you?"

"We're acquainted. I don't know him. We're not friends. I mean, we're not not friends. I just don't know him that well on a personal level."

"So how are you acquainted with him?"

"Well, everyone knows Nick. And I've seen him and talked to him plenty of times at the events he does. When he's dressed up as Santa. Nick's a fixture around town."

"Got it. For how long have you been acquainted with him in that capacity?"

"Oh, I don't know. Fifteen years at least."

"So how many times have you personally seen him and/ or interacted with him when he was hired to play Santa at various town functions?"

"I couldn't say. There have been many."

"More than ten?"

"Sure."

"More than twenty?"

"I'd say."

"Fifty times?"

"Maybe. If I had to guess. Less than fifty but more than thirty."

"I understand. Detective Haney, in all those times you've seen or interacted with Nick Whittaker when he was in costume playing Santa, have you ever known him to wear a beard wig?"

"What?"

"Well, he's sitting right here in this courtroom. You can look at him. He has a full, thick, naturally white beard, didn't he?"

"Well, yes."

"He's never worn a beard wig as far as you know, has he?"

Detective Haney looked at Lucky Braunlin. Then he looked back at me.

"Not that I recall, no. But at the same time, I can't say that I ever made a point of really paying much attention to the details of his costume."

"Right," I said. "Except when you were so certain that you could identify it from a grainy surveillance video."

That last bit was a risk. A comment I probably should have kept to myself until closing arguments. But it rattled Mark Haney. His eyes narrowed to slits.

"Detective, you're aware that Steve Anspaugh serves on the township zoning board, aren't you?"

"Of course."

"And in that capacity, Mr. Anspaugh has the power to grant or deny certain zoning variances for land held within the township, isn't that right?"

"That's correct."

"Are you also aware of a particularly contentious vote the township held regarding a variance requested by Amos Barnett?"

"What does that have to do with anything?"

"Please answer the question."

"I know Amos has some property he wants to develop and has run into some issues with the township."

"How did you become aware of that?"

"I just know it."

"You know Amos Barnett?"

"Sure."

"You're friends with Amos Barnett, aren't you? You're hunting buddies, in fact, isn't that right?"

"We've hunted together, yes."

"In fact, it's common knowledge around town that Amos Barnett has a particular beef with Steven Anspaugh regarding his vote to deny Mr. Barnett a zoning variance for the property he wanted to develop, isn't that right?"

"I can't answer to common knowledge."

"Right," I said. "But you can answer with your own personal knowledge, can't you?"

"Of course."

"So I'll ask this again. You were personally aware of Amos Barnett's displeasure with Steve Anspaugh over his vote to deny Barnett's variance, isn't that right?"

"I know Amos didn't like Steve. Yes."

I paused, letting his answer hang there for a moment. "Detective, you never bothered to question Amos Barnett in connection with this investigation, did you?"

Haney scowled but didn't answer.

"Detective, you never bothered to explore any other potential suspects who may have had a motive to do Steven Anspaugh harm, did you?"

"I didn't have to. I had physical evidence tying your client to the crime."

"That's a yes? You never questioned Amos Barnett. You never questioned anyone else who had a legitimate beef against Steve Anspaugh based on his voting record or anything else, did you?"

"Do I have to answer that?" Haney asked.

"Yes," Judge Homer said.

"I didn't question Barnett," Haney admitted.

"Thank you," I said.

I'd left a loose end regarding Nick's alibi. But there was very little I could accomplish on that with Haney. I'd have to find another way to answer that question for the jury. Still, there was one last thing I could do with Mark Haney.

"One more question, Detective," I said. "You only found wig fibers on the victim, is that your testimony? You didn't find hairs that didn't belong to him, did you?"

"What? No. No hairs."

"No natural white beard hairs?"

"No, ma'am," he answered, though he bit out that word ma'am.

"Thank you. I have no further questions at this time."

"Any redirect, Mr. Braunlin?"

"No. But I reserve the right to recall the detective on rebuttal." Lucky Braunlin barely looked up from his notes.

"All right then. We're adjourned until after lunch. Be ready with your next witness, Mr. Braunlin."

With that, I turned and walked back to the defense table. For the first time since I met him, Nick Whittaker gave me a genuine smile.

Chapter 13

"THE STATE CALLS Emily Connor to the stand, Your Honor."

Emily Connor couldn't have looked more like a stereotypical librarian if she tried. She wore her brown hair in a traditional bun, sported a floral print dress, and had a pair of wire-rimmed readers complete with a silver chain. She gave the jury a bright smile as she took her oath and situated herself in the witness box.

"Mrs. Connor," Braunlin started. "Let's cut right to it. Can you share with the jury what you remember about the night of July 25th of this year?"

Emily gripped the microphone with both hands before she spoke. For a moment, it looked like she was about to break into song. Then she pulled it down, angling it right at her mouth, and proceeded to answer a question she hadn't been asked.

"Seven years ago, I started doing a Christmas in July story time for the little kids. We'd read *A Night Before Christmas* and I put up a tree. Had an ornament-making contest, that sort of thing. I asked Mr. Whittaker to make an appearance, you know, dressed as Santa. I couldn't pay him, of course, but he didn't ask for money. That's one thing I could always count on. Mr. Whittaker was always happy to donate his time for things like that. Anyway, it got pretty popular. So maybe five years ago some of the other local businesses joined in. Putting decorations up, running sales, that kinda thing. Well, before you know it, it turned into a full-blown, week-long celebration."

"That's wonderful. But if we could focus on this past July 25th ..." Braunlin interjected, sensing both I and the judge were about to throw a flag.

"Oh, I'm getting to that," Emily said. "I just figured you could use some context. Anyway, this past July 25th was fixed to be the biggest event of all. For the past couple of years, we've been doing a gift exchange for the little ones. Local businesses donate money and toys. It's me and a couple of volunteers. We call ourselves the library elves. Anyway, we throw a Christmas party at the library in the commons. It's catered now. I think just about everybody in town comes to it. And Nick, he's the highlight. He comes out and passes out the gifts. We've got a velvet throne and everything for him to sit on. The kids get their pictures taken. They get candy canes. And he passes out the presents. It's great fun. Well, this year, it was all the same. You know, except for bigger."

"What time did Nick's part start?"

"He was there starting at six. Right when the party started. We were supposed to go from six to ten. After the library's normal hours. Nick was such a trooper. He always is. He takes ten-minute breaks every hour, but other than that, he's in that chair passing out presents and posing for pictures. The kids love it. Heck, so do the grown-ups."

"Was there anything unusual about this year's Christmas in July party at the library?"

"You mean what happened to Mr. Anspaugh? I'd say that was unusual."

"Well, yes, but let's focus on before that. I mean at the party itself."

"Well ... I'll be honest. I picked up on some tension with Nick and Mr. Anspaugh."

"How so?"

"You know about Nick's Christmas light show out at his house. I mean, everyone does. See, the way I heard it the zoning board was gonna have to put it to a vote to see if he could keep doing it. I'll be honest. I thought that was just a formality. I mean, who wouldn't want that light show to keep going? We all love it."

"Your Honor," I finally said. "Far be it from me to interrupt here, but so far the witness hasn't answered a single direct question."

Judge Homer waved a hand. "Mrs. Connor, I know you do love to tell your stories. And you're good at it. But Mrs. Leary is correct. In this courtroom, you need to answer just what you're asked."

"Well, that can't possibly be very interesting for them," she said, gesturing toward the jury. A few of them suppressed their laughter behind their hands. She was charming. It would make her a tricky witness on cross.

"Mrs. Connor," Braunlin said. "Here's my question. Did you notice anything unusual going on between Mr. Anspaugh and Mr. Whittaker that night?"

"You're talking about the argument I overheard?"

"Yes. Tell me about that."

"Oh, it was a shocker. I'd never heard Nick raise his voice before, much less the things he said."

"Tell me where you were. Tell me exactly what you overheard and how you came to overhear it."

She fidgeted with her sleeve, pulling out a perfectly folded square tissue. She blew her nose then put the tissue in her lap.

"We were running out of plastic cups for the punch bowl. I went to the break room to get some. When I came out, Nick and Mr. Anspaugh were standing in the hallway yelling at each other. Well, more Mr. Whittaker was yelling at Mr. Anspaugh."

"Did you hear what was being said?"

"Nick said, you can't do this. You can't take this away from me. Oh, and he was all red-faced. Jabbing his finger in Mr. Anspaugh's chest. Mr. Anspaugh tried to back away from him, but he was up against the wall. It concerned me because Nick is so much larger in stature than Mr. Anspaugh. He's maybe five inches taller and outweighs him by I'd say fifty pounds at least."

"Sure. Were you able to hear what Mr. Anspaugh was saying in response to this?"

"Not much. He was just shocked-looking. White-faced. His jaw was on the floor, so to speak. I think he told Nick to calm down once or twice. Nick said Mr. Anspaugh was going to ruin his life. He said he had no idea what this whole thing would do to him. He never really let Mr. Anspaugh get a word in edgewise."

"What did you do?"

"Do?"

"Did you intervene?"

"Oh no. I know better than to get in between two grown men with their dander up like that. But I was concerned. I thought maybe I'd go find Trudy Anspaugh, Mr. Anspaugh's wife. But that's when George and Mildred Rapp rounded the corner. They stopped in their tracks too. I mean, this is how loud Nick Whittaker was yelling. I kind of made eye contact with Mildred. You know. Neither of us knew what to do. But then Nick just kind of backed off. He walked away looking really defeated, head hanging low, shoulders slumped."

"Do you know what time this was?"

"Not the precise time, no. But it was after we did the tree lighting and before Nick said goodbye to the kids. So eight thirty at the latest. Nick was very specific that he wanted to be out by nine fifteen. He needed to get back home. He does this thing during the light show. Comes out and waves at everybody. He'd told me he wanted to make sure he got back in plenty of time to run everything over at his house."

"Did you talk to Nick after this altercation with Steve Anspaugh?"

"No."

"Did you see Nick Whittaker afterward?"

"I kind of lost track of him. I had a few things I had to be on top of myself. We had cookie decorating going on in one of the reading rooms. I took the cups back to the punch station and went to the reading room. And that's where I stayed until Trudy Anspaugh came back screaming."

"When was that?"

"Oh, that was late. After the party officially ended. A quarter past ten, I'd say. She'd come up a few minutes before that and asked me if I'd seen her husband. She said they were going to meet out at the car. You know Trudy. She's a master of the Irish goodbye. If Steve told her to make her rounds, it was gonna take her an hour to get to everybody. Anyway, she was going to go out to the car because she hadn't seen him for a while and she said something about knowing he probably went out there to sneak a cigarette. That's a bugaboo between them. He's been smoking for years, tells her he quits, but it's kind of a running joke through town. Everybody knows Steve Anspaugh smokes except his wife. Well, anyway, she went out to look for him. That had to be around ten I'd say because I was just about to start locking the doors. People were leaving. Then, a few minutes later, Trudy came in screaming bloody murder. She said to call 9-1-1. She said Steve's had an accident."

"Who else was there at the time?"

"It was me. The Rapps, George was helping me lock up. And he ran out there with Trudy. Mildred had her cell phone on her and she's the one who called the police. Well, when George came back, he looked white as a sheet. He came in just making sure we'd called for an ambulance. Then he ran back out there. I ran with him. That's when I saw poor Steve Anspaugh lying on his side, bleeding from his head."

"What happened next?"

"You know, it's all kind of a jumble. I got a hold of Trudy. She was hysterical by that point. Mildred wasn't much better. But I'd say it took maybe five or seven minutes before the ambulance came. Trudy went with them and one of the EMTs, Lonny

Crumpton. Well, Lonny told me and the Rapps to go back in the building and wait for the police to come. So that's what we did. Deputy Short came first. He'd actually been at the party earlier for a few minutes. His wife brought their little girl. Then Detective Haney came. He asked me about the parking lot cameras. In all the excitement, I'd completely forgotten we had them. I'm so glad he was on the ball. So I showed him the footage and the rest is history."

"Thank you, Mrs. Connor, that's all I have for you."

Emily Connor fixed her smile back in place as I took my position at the lectern.

"Mrs. Connor, I just want to clarify a few things. You never heard Mr. Whittaker say he was going to hurt Mr. Anspaugh, did you?"

"Hurt him? No. He didn't say that."

"And when you overheard this argument between them, you came up on it after it was already in progress, right? You didn't hear what started it?"

"Didn't need to. Nick was pretty clear on why he was mad."

"Be that as it may, you never heard what Steve Anspaugh said to Nick Whittaker before Mr. Whittaker said you can't take this away from me, right?"

"I didn't hear Steve's side of it, no. Nick was so loud though, I don't suppose I would have."

"Got it. So did Nick Whittaker come to the library already in costume or did he change when he was there?"

"He came in costume."

"He comes through the front door of the library?"

"Oh no, ma'am. He'd never do that. I let him in and out through the side door where we take deliveries. He drives a big old pickup truck and he wouldn't want the kids to see him pulling up in it. Spoils the illusion, you know?"

"Of course. And are there security cameras pointed at that side door, the delivery entrance?"

"No. Just the one in the parking lot we share with Township Hall. That way we can see who's coming in and out of the main entrances."

"So when Nick Whittaker came and left, it would have been through the side entrance, not the front."

"That's right."

"Did you see Nick leave? I mean, when he left the party for good?"

"No. He said goodbye to me while I was helping the kids in the reading room. Poked his head in. But I didn't actually see him leave."

"What way was he headed?"

"Toward the side."

"Toward the service entrance?"

"Right."

"Was there anyone else down that hallway?"

"Not that I know of. You have to go through an employee-only door."

"Is that kept locked?"

"No. Not while I'm there. But I lock up when I leave."

"Got it. So I'm clear. When Nick Whittaker left through the service entrance, there were no cameras that would have captured that, right?"

"That's right."

"Okay. Thank you. I have no further questions."

"None for me. Thanks, Mrs. Connor," Braunlin said.

As soon as Emily Connor stepped down, Lucky Braunlin called Russ Garfield to the stand.

Russ's testimony was brief. He'd been recording video outside Nick Whittaker's house the night of July 25th. He'd brought his twin daughters, Gracie and Lacey, aged six, to see the light show. He'd parked in the front row of the church parking lot.

Braunlin introduced Mr. Garfield's cell phone footage. The jury was treated to about sixty seconds of dancing lights to *Rudolph the Red-Nosed Reindeer*. Then *Up on the Housetop* started. That song repeated twice. Right after, *Jolly Old Saint Nicholas* played. Toward the end of the song, the spotlight shone on Nick's front door and he emerged in full Santa regalia, waving to the crowd.

"Mr. Garfield," Braunlin said. "Can you read the timestamp on the video you took?"

"I started recording at ten twenty-two. The video ends at ten twenty-seven right after Santa waved."

Braunlin played it a second time.

"How long did you sit watching the light show?"

"We got there at nine forty-five. The girls' bedtime in the summer is nine o'clock. But we read on social media that Santa would be making his appearance right at ten so I let them stay up to watch. They were getting pretty cranky when he didn't come out. I was going to leave but Gracie got upset. That set Lacey off and I knew I was outnumbered, so I waited. I texted my wife at ten fifteen to tell her why we weren't home. I told the girls if he's not out by ten thirty, that's that. So I was pretty glad he did finally show up."

"At ten twenty-seven, according to the time stamp on your video. So twenty-seven minutes late."

"Yep. That's an eternity when you've got two tired and cranky six-year-olds."

"I'll bet. Thank you, Mr. Garfield, that's all I have."

"All right," Judge Homer said. "You think you can finish up cross in the next half hour, Ms. Leary, or do we need to adjourn? It's past four already."

"I can finish up in five minutes or less, Your Honor," I said.

"Excellent."

I moved past Lucky Braunlin. "Mr. Garfield, if we can go back to the beginning of your video footage. What song is that playing again?"

I started the video and stopped it after ten seconds.

"That's *Rudolph.*"

"Right. It's a pretty incredible show, isn't it?"

"My girls love it."

"Me too. I had the pleasure of seeing it the other night. Have you taken the girls out this month?"

"Sure have. Twice. It's been a little tough to explain to them why Santa doesn't come out his front door anymore. But they still like the show."

"Which song's their favorite?" I asked, taking a stab in the dark.

"Oh, *Rudolph*, for sure."

"Why's that?"

"Because they get a kick out of it when Rudolph's nose lights up in time to the music."

"Yes. That's pretty cute. I think that's my favorite too. But that night, July 25th, Rudolph didn't light up during the song at all, did he? I mean, you can hear one of your daughters in the video asking you about it."

"Yeah. I don't know if he was having technical trouble or what. But Rudolph did finally light up."

"Not until the *Jolly Old Saint Nicholas* song though, right? Not until just before Santa finally came out the front door, right?"

"That's right."

"Got it. You said you were sitting in the church parking lot for almost forty-five minutes prior to that, right?"

"Right."

"Could you see anyone coming or going from Nick Whittaker's house?"

"You mean like pulling in or out? No. He's got a driveway that curves around the back. And when that light show is on, you can't really see much of anything else. It's too dark."

"So someone could have pulled in around the back, but you wouldn't have been able to see it?"

Garfield looked puzzled for a moment. "Yeah. No. I wasn't looking at anything but the lights. So I didn't try to see anything else. But it would have been pretty hard."

"Someone could have pulled in."

"They could have. Sure. Especially if they turned off their headlights."

"Thank you," I said. "No further questions from me."

"Good," Judge Homer said. "Then we're adjourned for the day. The jury is instructed not to discuss this case with anyone, including each other. And we'll see you here bright and early at eight o'clock tomorrow."

Judge Homer banged his gavel. I sat down next to Nick. I had a few minutes before the deputies would come to take him back to his cell.

"It went good?" he asked, his eyes hopeful. I put a hand over his.

"We're getting there, Nick. We're getting there."

I hoped I was right. But I knew Lucky Braunlin's best witness had yet to take the stand.

Chapter 14

I HAD ten minutes to talk to my client before the deputies had to take him back to his cell. As it was, they stood guard outside the door to the conference room across the hall from Judge Homer's chambers. Nick sat in a chair against the wall, head down, cuffed hands folded in his lap.

"They all believe it, don't they?" he said. "They all think I did that to Mr. Anspaugh. That I hurt him. How could they think I hurt him?"

"Some good things happened today, Nick. Some very good things. I've laid some groundwork that I'm hoping will pay off for us a little later."

"Mrs. Connor thinks I beat Steve Anspaugh. I saw it in her eyes. The way she looked at me. She's known me most of my life, Ms. Leary. If she thinks I could do that, it'll be too easy for the rest of them to believe that. You have to let me get up there and tell them what happened. I have to be able to explain."

I sat in the chair beside him. "We're not there yet. Mr. Braunlin still has a few more witnesses to call. Let me do my job."

Nick fixed his red-rimmed eyes on me. He seemed child-like almost. Defeated. "Please let me tell those people my side of the story. I can stand up to Mr. Braunlin. I know I can."

I wasn't so sure. In ninety-nine percent of the criminal cases I'd defended, putting the accused on the stand would have been a mistake. I hadn't yet decided whether Nick could do himself more harm than good.

"I'll tell you what," I said. "Let's table that decision until at least the end of the day tomorrow. Braunlin probably won't rest until the day after that. In the meantime, as much as you can, I need you to get a good night's sleep. Tomorrow is going to be even harder. We're going to hear from Mr. Anspaugh's doctor. There will be more crime scene photographs entered. Videos of Steve Anspaugh's injuries and condition. And Trudy Anspaugh will probably take the stand. It's going to be difficult for you not to react. Not to get angry. Just remember what I told you."

"You want me stoic," he whispered. "You want me to not show any anger even though these people are lying about me. They're all assuming the very worst of me even though I've been a friend to them my whole life."

I put a hand on Nick's back. It was easy to feel how Aimee Whittaker felt. Even though Nick was a grown man nearing sixty years old, he made you want to take care of him. To mother him.

"I really appreciate everything you're doing for me," he said. "I know it's hard. It's almost Christmas. I'm sure you need to get home to your own family. Your kids?"

"It's just me," I said. "No kids."

"Are you married?"

"No."

Nick considered me. "Maybe we're more alike than I thought. Do you have a big family otherwise?"

"It's big enough. I've got an older brother then a younger brother and sister. They've got kids."

"Where do you spend Christmas?"

"They all come to my house. It's kind of a tradition. Christmas on the lake."

"That sounds really peaceful."

I laughed. "Not exactly. You'd have to know my family. My older brother Joe and my younger brother Matty usually find something to argue with each other about. Joe's daughter Emma, she's grown now. She'll usually bring a new boyfriend and it ends up turning into a train wreck. My sister Vangie cooks. Not very well. Her daughter Jessa is nearly a teenager and acting like it. Matty and his girlfriend have a newborn. Then there are the dogs and various strays we take in."

"More dogs?"

"No. People. My law partner Jeanie had kind of adopted us. She's been a mother figure to my younger siblings. Me too, I guess."

"Your folks aren't in the picture?"

"Not anymore."

"I'm sorry for that."

I smiled. "I guess we do have more in common than I realized."

"It can be chaotic at Aimee's house too. Her kids. Their friends. I have other cousins too. They all rotate who has Christmas. They're good to me though. I don't know what I'd do without family, you know?"

"Me either."

The deputy poked his head in. "Sorry, Ms. Leary, we've got to transport."

"Of course. I'll see you first thing in the morning, Nick. We've got a lot of work ... a lot of fight ahead of us." I stopped myself just short of promising him that everything would be okay. It's the one thing I could never do.

Chapter 15

A LIGHT SNOW had started to fall by the time I drove to the Perpetual Hope Church. Just past six p.m. the sun had already set. We were just a couple of days off from the winter solstice, the shortest day of the year.

Dharma Till came out of the side door to the church. She pulled a thick, cable-knit cardigan tight around her waist to stave off the blast of cold air. She raised her hand in a wave.

"Hi, Dharma," I called out. I was tired. I wanted nothing more than to head to the little one-bedroom guest house alone and shut the door on the day's events. As much as I told Nick to get a good night's sleep, I needed one too. But a heavenly scent wafted toward me as Dharma closed the door behind her.

"Cass," she said, breathless as she walked up to my car. "You're just in time. I made a pot roast with redskin potatoes and some baby carrots. There's way too much for just Richard and I to eat. Please join us. I know you've probably got a million things running through your mind. But you have to eat, right?"

I didn't have a good argument. I also didn't have dinner plans and the thought of getting takeout delivered again made my stomach roll.

"That's very generous of you," I said.

"Good!" Dharma said brightly; she looped her arm through mine. I barely had a chance to hit the lock button on my key fob before she pulled me along with her into the church.

Sure enough, the delicious scent of Dharma's pot roast made my stomach growl.

I followed Dharma into the small kitchen down the hall. She had a huge roasting pan sitting on top of the stove. There looked to be enough food to feed the entire congregation. Dharma had already set the table for three. She gestured for me to sit on the opposite end of the table. Before I could offer to help her, Dharma lifted the giant roasting pan and set it in the center of the table. She then busied herself carving up slices of thick, fall-off-the-bone beef. She served me a generous helping with potatoes, onions, and carrots, and poured some of the juices over it from the bottom of the pan.

"This looks delicious," I said, reaching for the carafe filled with ice water and pouring myself a glass.

The meat was so tender, I didn't even need my knife.

"Do you want to talk about it?" Dharma said. She filled her own plate and one more for the reverend. As if on cue, he came around the hallway and joined us at the kitchen table. He leaned over and kissed his wife on the cheek while spreading his napkin over his lap and sitting across from me.

"Leave her alone, Dharma, Cass probably wants to shut her brain off for the day."

"It's all right," I said. "Actually, I wouldn't mind getting both your input on what I might be able to expect from some of tomorrow's witnesses."

"I heard Emily Connor didn't do poor Nick any favors," Reverend Rich said.

"You heard that already?" I asked.

He shrugged. "Dale Hanover was in the courtroom. He works for the local paper. I ran into him at the post office a little while ago."

"Emily saw what she thinks she saw," Dharma said. "She's a good person. She's just very close to Trudy Anspaugh. She was the first one to get to her after ... well ... you know ... after she saw poor Steve like that."

"Trudy's probably going to testify tomorrow," I said. "How well do either of you know her? She wouldn't talk to me. Wouldn't return my calls."

"She's scared," Rich offered. "Trudy's a good-hearted woman, but Steve was her whole world."

"He took care of her," Dharma said. "They live in this beautifully remodeled farmhouse off Church Road. It's on ten acres. Hundred-year-old oaks and maples. But Steve does everything to maintain it. He never wanted her to lift a finger. Now, she doesn't know how. She's lost."

"You've ministered to her?" I asked Reverend Rich.

"On occasion. She hasn't come to see me recently. To be honest, I think seeing Nick's house upsets her too much. And now with the light show on every night, I think it scares her."

"So Trudy has no doubt that Nick's the one who did this to her husband?"

Dharma and Rich exchanged a look. Dharma put her fork down. "I'm sorry, Cass. Trudy's not going to do Nick any favors on the witness stand."

"I appreciate your thoughts."

"I don't know how helpful they are," Dharma said.

"They're very helpful. It gives me at least some clue what to expect from her. I'll approach her gently. I would have anyway, but understanding a bit of the dynamic between Trudy and Steve really is helpful."

We ate in companionable silence for a few minutes. Then Dharma dropped her fork to her plate and put a hand over her eyes. Rick reached across the table and put a hand on his wife's arm.

"I'm sorry," Dharma sniffled. "I just don't understand how everything got so terrible. I never would have believed Nick Whittaker could harm so much as a spider."

"Do you think he did?" I asked.

She shook her head. "No. I don't think so. But who else?"

"That's really what I'm trying to figure out. I know Steve Anspaugh wasn't the most popular man in town, especially to business owners."

"But he's not the only one," Dharma said. "The zoning board has four people on it, not just Steve."

"About that. Everyone is assuming Steve Anspaugh was going to vote against Nick. Do you have any idea if that's true? Has there been any gossip or loose talk from the other members of the board?"

Richard raised a brow. "Well, of all of them, Terrence Fitz and Steve Anspaugh were probably the closest. They played in a golf league together. That said, I can't imagine Fitz or anyone else talking out of turn, you know? They act like it's an issue of national security."

"Fitz is on Lucky Braunlin's witness list," I said. "I expect he'll take the stand tomorrow."

Dharma threw her napkin down. "Oh, it's just so stupid. Nobody cares! Everyone wants those Christmas lights. Nick's not even there anymore and people are still coming."

Dharma got up from her seat. She went over to the window and pulled up the shades. Sure enough, cars were beginning to line up on the west side of the parking lot. In a few more minutes, the show would start.

Rich left his seat. He went to his wife's side and put an arm around her. She cried softly into his shoulder.

I felt like an intruder. An interloper during an intimate moment between a husband and wife.

"I think it says something that they haven't even bothered to bring it to a vote in all these months," Dharma said. "I know it's terrible of me to say, but I'm angry at Steve Anspaugh. I just ... am."

"Dharma," Rich said. "He's the victim in this, no matter what else he may be."

"I know that. But Steve stirred trouble with this for no reason. Why now? Why after all these years did there need to be some kind of formal variance for some Christmas lights?"

"It's what Nick doesn't understand either," I said. I left my seat and cleared my plate. By the time I finished, Dharma and Rich had come away from the window.

"I really appreciate your hospitality, tonight and every night. It means a lot to Nick as well. He wants you to know that."

"We're glad to help," Reverend Rich said. "In fact, there's something I wanted to give you. Can you wait here for a moment?"

I walked to the window and watched across the street with Dharma. A moment later, Nick's light show began. There were fewer cars out there tonight, but it was still early.

Reverend Rich came back a few minutes later. He had a long white envelope in his hand. He gave it to me.

"It's not much," he said. "But it means so much to the congregation. And to Dharma and me."

The envelope wasn't sealed. I opened it. In it was a check for two thousand dollars made out to me. In the memo line, Rich had written, "Nick Whittaker's Legal Defense Fund."

"Reverend, this is extremely generous."

"It's a drop in the bucket, I suspect. You're defending a man against a possible life sentence, aren't you? And you're far outside the jurisdiction you normally practice. I'd imagine your fee is probably three times that or more."

"I appreciate it," I said.

"You have overhead," Dharma said. "Employees, an investigator, right? Like Rich says, it's a drop in the bucket."

"Thank you," I said. I'd leaned my messenger bag against the wall. I picked it up and slipped the envelope into the leather portfolio I kept in the outside compartment.

"I've taken up enough of your time," I said. "Thank you for dinner and for your insights. And for this." I patted the outside compartment.

"I can walk you back to the guest house," Rich said. "It's dark out there now."

"I'm fine," I said. "It's just across the parking lot."

"Well, you holler if you need anything," Rich said. "Is the furnace kicking out enough heat for you?"

"It's perfectly toasty," I said. I slipped my coat back on and headed out the side door. The snow had picked up. Fat, fluffy, flakes coated me within seconds. I watched my steps as I made my way down the curved walk. There was just a small path separating the church parking lot from the walkway up to the guest house.

I reached into my coat pocket and felt for the key Dharma had given me. A motion light came on as I got closer to the door.

It was then I saw movement through the barren trees. I froze.

A shadowy figure stood just inside the tree line. He wore a dark, puffy coat and a ski mask. A pair of yellow eyes glared at me through the slits in the mask.

"Who's there?" I called out, adrenaline coursing through me. I remembered what Eric taught me. Look for an out. Which way could I run?

The man was behind me, slightly to my right. I'd have to go past him to get to the front door of the guest house. No good. Running into the woods was no option. That only left going back the way I came, toward the church, toward the dozens of cars parked along the west side, currently all facing the other direction. Would anyone hear me if I screamed?

"Who's there?" I called out. "You know I can see you. You know there are surveillance cameras all over this property." A bluff, but hopefully an effective one.

The figure advanced on me. He had his hands stuffed in his pockets. I swore I saw a bulge on the right side.

Don't panic. Don't panic. Don't panic.

I turned on my heel and started to run. I got about two steps before running smack into a wall of muscle.

I slipped in the snow and landed hard on my rear end.

"Get on out of here!" Reverend Rich Till yelled. "I see you! What do you think you're doing out there, boy? You're on private property!"

Rich reached down and helped me to my feet. The masked figure bolted sideways and started to run. A tree branch caught his jacket. He flailed his arms trying to free himself. In the process, his ski mask came off.

"A.J.?" Reverend Rich called out. "Amos Jr.! I see you. I told you, you need to go on home!"

Rich helped me to my feet. "Good heavens, are you all right? I came out here to warn you. I salted but it's still slick."

I looked back toward the running figure of A.J. Barnett, Amos Barnett's son.

"He was ... he was watching us. Watching me," I said, my heart still pounding out of my chest.

"Are you okay?" Dharma had come outside. She yelled across the parking lot.

"We're okay!" Rich yelled back. "Go back inside, honey."

Rich hooked a hand under my elbow. He had a flashlight in his free hand. He turned it on and lit the rest of our way up the sidewalk.

"Thank you," I said. "I don't know ... he was just ..."

"A.J.'s a good kid. Normally. I'll talk to Amos and see if everything's all right out there. A.J. didn't have any business prowling around out there tonight. I hope I didn't scare him too badly. He might have just been looking for some fellowship."

I kept my thoughts to myself. Spying on women from the woods while wearing a ski mask didn't seem particularly Christian. But maybe Reverend Rich was right. Still, after I stepped inside the guest house, I locked the door behind me and pulled down every window shade. There was something going on with A.J. Barnett all right. I knew in my soul it wasn't something good.

Chapter 16

"You gotta understand, we weren't planning to take this action lightly."

Terrence Fitz looked like he might get physically sick right there on the witness stand. He came in wearing an honest-to-goodness Fedora which he currently clasped between his hands. The odds of it ever taking the right shape again dwindled every minute.

"Of course not." Lucky Braunlin leaned against the far end of the jury box. Away from the microphone at the lectern, he had to shout to be heard. "But how can you be so certain that Steve Anspaugh, your colleague on the Helene Township Zoning Board, was leaning toward denying the variance Nick Whittaker needed?"

"Because he told me," Fitz said. "We discussed it. We all did. Me. Steve. Delores Flax. All of us. Look. I'm not gonna sit up here and say I haven't enjoyed what Mr. Whittaker has tried to do out there. They call him the Christmas Guy, you know? I'm aware ... we were all aware that voting down his variance had the potential to have us all labeled as Scrooges or Grinches or whatever other names people wanted to throw. But we work for the township as a whole, not just one man. There are other issues to consider."

"Certainly," Braunlin said. "But what I'm asking you today, do you know whether Steve Anspaugh actually told Nick Whittaker he was planning to vote down his variance?"

"Objection," I said. "The question invites hearsay, Your Honor."

"Sustained," Judge Homer said. "Mr. Braunlin, that's the third time we've gone down this road. Mr. Fitz simply cannot answer questions about what Mr. Anspaugh says he said to somebody else."

Braunlin pushed himself off the jury box. He paced for a moment in front of it, then finally made his way back to the lectern.

"Mr. Fitz, answer me this then. How were you planning on voting? Were you inclined to grant Mr. Whittaker his variance or not?"

"Objection," I said. "Relevance."

"Your Honor, I think the mood at the time of the attack on Mr. Anspaugh is relevant."

"Mood isn't an element of the crime, Your Honor," I said.

"She's right, Mr. Braunlin. I'm sustaining that objection as well."

"Fine," Braunlin said. "I'll withdraw the question. Your witness, Ms. Leary."

Braunlin shook his head as he made his way back to his table. I stood up at mine and faced the witness.

"Mr. Fitz, I appreciate how difficult this must be for you. Steve Anspaugh is your friend, isn't he?"

"He was. Yes. Um. He is."

"You're very close, aren't you?"

"We're close. I've known Steve since we were kids. We played on the same Little League team. His parents lived two streets down from mine growing up. Steve's the one who talked me into running for a seat on the zoning board."

"And even though it's been almost six months since his hospitalization, you haven't taken any steps to replace him on the zoning board, have you?"

"What? No. No. I can't even think about that right now. None of us can. Not until ... well ... we're just hoping for some closure. Some resolution to all of this. It's been hard to move on."

"Of course. Helene is a very tight-knit community. I can see that."

"We are. You have to understand how awful this has been for everybody. And just ... seeing Trudy around town. Well, it breaks my heart is what."

I let Fitz take a few breaths and compose himself before I asked my next question.

"It's not an easy job you have, is it? The zoning board?"

"I don't know what you mean?"

"Well, I mean you can't please everyone, can you?"

"Oh, people have their opinions about our work, that's for sure. But we strive to do what's best for the community as a whole. People get the wrong idea about Steve. He gets labeled as anti-development. Anti-growth. But we have something very special here in Helene. You're new to town. Tell me you don't know what I'm talking about?"

An odd thing, having a witness start to ask me questions. But it suited my purposes for the moment and neither Judge Homer nor Lucky Braunlin did anything to stop it.

"Oh, you have a wonderful community here. It's like stepping back in time in a lot of ways. Clean streets. Immaculate downtown area. Neighbors helping neighbors. I've witnessed a lot of that myself. In fact, I've been shown nothing but hospitality since I got here. And that's saying something. It's not always easy being an outsider."

"We don't think that way at all," Fitz said. "Not at all. We understand how much tourism brings to Helene. It's just ... it's our duty to make sure everything that's done, every new business or request for a variance ... it's gotta be granted sparingly and in keeping with the township plan."

"Certainly. But let me circle back to something you said. Steve Anspaugh, among all of you on the board, he was ... I'm sorry ... is considered a hard-liner, isn't he?"

"What do you mean?"

"Well, I mean, isn't it true that the consensus around town is that Steve Anspaugh's the one to convince if you want something changed? In other words, if you can convince Anspaugh, the rest of the board tends to follow?"

"We all have equal voting power, ma'am. But yes. Steve's been on the zoning board the longest. We all hold a lot of respect for his opinions."

"He's made enemies over the years, hasn't he?"

Fitz started to look uncomfortable. He squeezed his poor hat into a tube.

"I don't like to think about that," he said.

"I know. It's difficult. But I'm going to need you to. Isn't it true that a member of this town threatened Steve Anspaugh after a controversial vote?"

"I don't condone that sort of thing."

"Neither do I. But you know who I'm talking about, don't you?"

"I know the sheriff had words with Amos Barnett. He showed up after a board meeting one night, drunk, waving his fists, swearing up a storm. He got in Steve's face."

"He'd applied for a variance on sixty acres of property-zoned residential off of Mallard Road, isn't that right?"

"I believe so, yes."

"You believe or you know? You were a member of the panel who voted Mr. Barnett down, aren't you?"

"Barnett took the vote pretty hard. I'll admit that. He made his displeasure known, that's true. But if you're insinuating that Amos Barnett had anything ..."

"Mr. Fitz, I'm not insinuating anything. I'm simply asking you if you're aware, from personal knowledge, that Amos Barnett harbored ill will against Steve Anspaugh after your zoning board refused to grant his variance."

"He did, yes."

"Did Mr. Barnett ever threaten you or get in your face?"

"What? No."

"That sixty acres out on Mallard, it's still sitting vacant and unused, isn't it?"

"As far as I know. You'd have to ask Amos."

"But surely you drive by it every day on your way into town, don't you? You've seen the For Sale signs on it."

"Yes."

"Almost a million dollars, that's what Mr. Barnett paid for that property, isn't it?"

"I believe so, yes."

"And you personally heard Mr. Barnett threaten Steve Anspaugh, didn't you?"

"Amos wasn't his best self. He'd been drinking. People say things in the heat of passion sometimes."

"What did Amos say?"

"Objection," Lucky Braunlin said. "If this witness can't testify about what Anspaugh said to the defendant, he certainly can't testify about what Amos Barnett said to Anspaugh."

"Your Honor, in this case, the threat I'm speaking of isn't offered to prove the truth of the matter asserted. I'm offering it simply to establish that Mr. Fitz heard it."

"The witness can answer whether he heard a threat being made," Judge Homer said. "But Mr. Fitz, I'll ask you to refrain from repeating what it was you heard. You can't testify to it word for word."

"Amos threatened Anspaugh. That's true. But that was years ago."

"Threatened him," I said. "With bodily harm, isn't that right?"

"He said he was going to ..."

"Objection!"

"Sorry," Fitz said. "Yes. Amos said something that I would construe as a threat to physically hurt Steve. But I'm telling you, he didn't take it seriously."

"Thank you," I said. "And Mr. Fitz, isn't it true that Steve Anspaugh ran afoul of several other developers over the years who had commercial designs on plats of land throughout the township?"

"Oh, people have been trying to develop that strip of land off Mallard Road for years. It's easy on and off from US 31. But it's not gonna happen on my watch. Not Steve's either."

"And every time you vote to deny variances or new development, you make enemies, isn't that right?"

"That's a strong word."

"But accurate?"

"Well, we can't always make friends, no."

"Mr. Fitz, did Detective Haney ever talk to you in connection with his investigation into the assault on Steve Anpaugh?"

"No."

"To your knowledge did he interview the other members of the zoning board?"

"I don't think so, no."

"Did he ever ask for records of past votes? Particularly those that went against Mr. Barnett or other land developers?"

"No."

"Thank you," I said. "I have nothing further."

"Mr. Braunlin, any redirect?"

"No, Your Honor."

"All right. Then we're adjourned until after lunch. Tell your next witness to be ready at one on the dot, Mr. Braunlin."

I already knew who that would be. Lucky Braunlin planned to call Dr. Noah Charles. His testimony would be graphic and devastating.

Nick looked defeated as the deputies took him back to holding. I would have sat with him, but I had a phone call to make.

I gathered my things and found a quiet spot in an alcove of the courthouse basement. As long as my cell phone signal held, this would be my go-to hideaway for the duration of the trial.

Eric answered on the second ring. In the background I could hear carolers singing.

"Where are you?" I asked.

"It's my mother's choir," he answered. "They're practicing in the other room. Let me close the door. I'm glad you called. I've got a couple of things for you."

One of the court clerks walked past me. She seemed startled to see me, but found a smile as she hustled past, clutching a file folder to her chest.

"I hope it's good news," I said.

"Well, your victim is about as clean as they come. Can't find so much as a parking ticket on him. Same goes for your client."

"Anspaugh's ruffled the usual feathers in his tenure on the zoning board down here. I managed to get that out before the lunch break. It's serious straw-grasping though."

"It only takes one straw for reasonable doubt, Cass. You'll get it. I know you."

"Thanks for the vote of confidence. But what about Anspaugh's financials? Anything there?"

"He owns his house outright. No mortgage. Perfect credit score. Jeanie's working on the wife's financial picture. But so far, everything's coming back squeaky clean. Same with your guy. He's not rich or anything, but he pays his taxes and stays out of trouble."

"Right. What about the other name I texted you? Amos Barnett?"

"He's under water. There are tax liens on three of his properties. A couple of DUIs. He was arrested for malicious destruction of property and menacing a few years back. Did you get that in today?"

"More or less, yes. The jury is aware he's no fan of Steve Anspaugh's. But Braunlin's going to be telling them that's old news. It's been years since the board denied his variance. He's going to question why this came to a head now."

"I'm sorry, Cass. I wasn't able to find anything recent on Barnett but I'm not done looking. If you give me a little more time, I'll see what I can dig up. It's like you said. His troubles seemed to be several years ago."

"And Aimee Whittaker says there've been no bites on his vacant land in almost two years. It's not like he just had something fall through. It's just ... the way he acted when he saw me out there. And last night ..."

"Cass? What about last night? Did this guy come after you? I don't like it. If you're standing there in open court and accusing him of this crime, you're the one who's likely to stoke him to anger. If he's resorted to violence in the past."

"Relax. I'm just asking questions. I'm not in the guy's face or anything."

"You don't have to be. What about last night?"

"What?" I regretted saying it. I hoped maybe Eric would forget. No such luck.

"You said last night. What happened?"

"Nothing. Nothing you need to worry about. It's just ... Barnett's teenage kid was lurking around the church. Reverend Till ran him off."

"His kid. How old's this kid?"

"I don't know. Fifteen, maybe? Sixteen? He's just a kid."

"Cass, I don't have to tell you. I know I don't have to tell you. Be careful. You don't know these people. You've stepped into a mess of local politics and trouble you don't know the history of. What's this kid's name?"

"Eric, he's a kid."

"His name, Cass."

I sighed. "Amos Junior."

"Got it. I'll see what I can find out."

"See if you can find anything out about Barnett's ex-wife. Sadie Barnett. She left Helene years ago. If she's out there somewhere, I wouldn't mind talking to her. And on Amos Junior, he's a juvenile. His records will be sealed. I don't know what you'll be able to find."

"You let me worry about that. Just promise me you're being careful."

"Always. Stop worrying about me."

"Never," he said and it made me smile. "I just wish I could get up there and help you."

"You are helping me. And your parents need you right now more than I do. I'll be home in a couple of days."

"Not soon enough. I miss you."

"I miss you too."

"All right. I'll call you tomorrow. Stay safe. And thank the reverend for me. Tell him he's got my permission to scare off whoever comes near you."

Shaking my head, I clicked off. Eric worried too much. I knew that would never change. The clock on the wall read 12:45. Lunchtime was over. It meant Lucky Braunlin's two most powerful witnesses were about to take the stand.

Chapter 17

"DR. CHARLES," Lucky Braunlin said. "Can you describe the extent of Steven Anspaugh's injuries to the jury?"

Noah Charles was the kind of witness juries loved. Handsome with a distinguished amount of salt and pepper through his thick, wavy hair. He wore a pair of black, horn-rimmed glasses that gave him that professorial air. He wore a three-piece suit, the style of which harkened back to the early eighties, but somehow he made it look fashionable. I knew my best play was to get him off the stand as quickly as I could if at any point he stopped being neutral.

"Mr. Anspaugh suffered severe trauma to the head and upper body. He had a comminuted frontal fracture and a right orbital floor fracture. In lay terms, the area above his right eye was broken in three places and the bone beneath his right eye was also fractured. In fact, a few millimeters up, and he probably would have lost that eye. There were of course several deep lacerations to his face and an avulsion on the back of his head at the crown. He had more minor, non-life-threatening injuries as well. A couple of broken ribs, his left wrist, and multiple contusions and lacerations on his arms and legs."

"You're describing a series of injuries that covered his entire body, aren't you?"

"I am, yes. This man was severely beaten for a prolonged amount of time."

One by one, Lucky Braunlin introduced photographs of Anspaugh's injuries. As the doctor described, he was bruised and beaten on nearly every part of his body. The head wounds were of course the worst to look at. His eye bulged out unnaturally in the photos taken close to his admission to the ER. The avulsion the doctor described to the back of his head was a giant flap and part of his skull could be seen. Other photographs taken a few days and weeks after the attack were in a lot of ways worse as the bruising settled in.

"Dr. Charles, would you describe this case as one of the worst beatings you've ever seen?"

"Objection, counsel is leading the witness," I said.

"Sustained. Try again, Mr. Braunlin."

Beside me, Nick started to weep. He buried his face in his hands. Every single juror turned their attention to him. I couldn't decide whether that was a good thing or not just yet.

"Doctor, can you give me an idea how bad a case this was, based on your experience?"

"As a neurologist, I specialize in trauma to the brain and spinal cord. As such, the majority of my caseload is made up of patients who've been injured in car accidents or falls. I've also treated many victims of violent crimes. Domestic violence makes up the majority of those. But I can tell you, in my twenty years in this specialty, Mr. Anspaugh's injuries would have to rank in probably the top five in terms of the severity and brutality. At least among those patients who've survived."

"Dr. Charles, I'd like to draw your attention to the injuries on Mr. Anspaugh's legs, arms, and hands. Can you hazard an educated guess as to how those were inflicted?"

"Well, particularly the bruising and lacerations to his hands. Those are consistent with defensive wounds."

"Meaning?"

"Meaning my patient was likely holding his hands and fists out and away from his face, trying to defend himself against the blows and beating he was taking."

"So he would have been conscious for much of the attack?"

"He would have been conscious, yes. Until his assailant delivered the blows to his head, the worst ones. The blows that fractured his skull would very likely have rendered him unconscious."

"Both of them? Just one of them?"

"It's hard to say. And it's also impossible to say whether Mr. Anspaugh might have simply passed out from pain or blood loss before those blows were delivered. We can't ever know."

"But it's possible that some of those blows to the head were delivered after Mr. Anspaugh had already stopped fighting or was unconscious?"

"Very possible."

"Almost a coup de grâce, you might say?"

"Objection," I said. "Calls for speculation and the question is outside the bounds of this witness's medical knowledge and expertise."

"I'll withdraw it," Braunlin said.

"Dr. Charles, what is Steven Anspaugh's prognosis today? He's in a coma, is he not?"

"Coma can mean a lot of things. He is in a reduced state of awareness. A minimally conscious state. And he has been, in essence, since July 25th, when he sustained these injuries. Initially, we kept him in a so-called medically induced coma while we tried to give his body time to heal. At the time, one of my biggest concerns, as it always is with injuries of this sort, is the build-up of intracranial pressure. Swelling in the brain."

"And how do you treat that?"

"We opened what we call burr holes to allow the brain to expand within the skull cavity without causing additional damage."

"You drilled holes into Mr. Anspaugh's skull."

"It's an inelegant way to describe it, but yes, essentially. And not me personally. My colleague, Dr. Robison, performed that procedure. I'm a neurologist. He's a neurosurgeon."

"What is Mr. Anspaugh's current level of function?"

"He is breathing on his own, that's the good news. He's showing improvement in his reflexes. He seems to respond to familiar people, though it's not entirely clear whether those responses are involuntary. But as I said, Mr. Anspaugh remains in a light coma."

"Will he wake up?"

"Well, wakefulness isn't just one state of being, you understand, so it's hard to ..."

"Will he recognize his family? Will he be able to talk again? Will he walk? Will he ever be able to feed himself again?"

"The simple answer is, I don't know. The brain is a complex organism. Mr. Anspaugh is showing small signs of improvement as time goes on. As I said, he does appear to make purposeful movements when family members or certain staff members on his care team are with him. Those instances are increasing with time. That is encouraging. He's not done healing. Where he is today versus where he might be six months from now? I can't say. But if you're asking me whether he'll ever recover fully and be the man he was before this assault? I would say no. That's impossible. In a best-case scenario, Mr. Anspaugh will probably always need medical care. To what extent? There's no way to tell."

"Thank you, Doctor. I have no further questions."

"Ms. Leary?"

There was little I could do with the good doctor that could help Nick Whittaker. For his part, Nick hadn't stopped crying from the moment Dr. Charles referred to the first photograph of Steven Anspaugh. But neither could I let him just leave the stand.

"Doctor," I said. "If I can take you back to the night Mr. Anspaugh was brought into the hospital. Were you consulted on the case right away?"

"I was involved, yes."

"You saw him."

"I saw him."

"These injuries, these ... horrific ... extensive injuries. Forgive me for asking something that might seem obvious, but these were the types of injuries that caused a large amount of blood loss, weren't they?"

"Oh, absolutely. Especially the wounds to his head. There was a massive amount of bleeding. Mr. Anspaugh lost almost half his blood volume that night. In addition to the intracranial pressure I described, the loss of blood was the second most life-threatening issue for him."

"I see. And in those photographs, Mr. Anspaugh was covered in his own blood, wasn't he?"

"Of course."

"These injuries were delivered at close range, weren't they?"

"I don't know what you mean?"

"I mean, whoever did this to him was in close personal contact with him. Again, I'm sorry if that seems like an obvious question."

"Yes," he said. "The attacker would have had to have had close personal contact with the victim. My understanding is that these injuries were made with a tire iron. I can't of course tell you whether the assailant actually made skin-to-skin contact with Mr. Anspaugh, but he would have been within inches of him when he swung that iron."

"And as you said, there was a lot of blood."

"Yes."

I tapped my fingers on the lectern. "One more thing. Has Mr. Anspaugh spoken at all in the five months since his admission to the hospital?"

"He's been verbal at times, but I wouldn't describe it as intelligent speech."

"Do you believe he's been trying to talk?"

"I think that's possible. What's impossible is knowing how aware he is. His level of cognition is not something we have the tools to accurately gauge. He can hear. He can see. He can feel. As I said, he responds to people and sounds. Certain types of music seem to calm him when he's agitated. But he cannot currently communicate in a way that we'd call normal or unimpaired."

"Thank you. I have no further questions."

"None from me, Your Honor," Braunlin said. With that, Dr. Charles stepped down and left the courtroom.

I went back to my seat. Nick was still crying. I handed him a tissue from the box on the table. He wiped his eyes and blew his nose so loudly it sounded like a strangled goose.

"Mr. Braunlin, are you ready to call your next witness?"

"Your Honor, may we approach the bench?"

I turned my attention away from Nick.

"You may. But make it quick," Judge Homer said.

I patted Nick on the back and walked up to the sidebar.

"Your Honor," Lucky said. "I was planning on closing out my case in chief after putting the victim's wife, Trudy Anspaugh, on the stand. Unfortunately, she's in no condition to give her testimony today."

"Why not?" Both the judge and I said it in unison.

"Well, she's just a wreck, is all. Nearly hysterical, if you want to know the truth. I just can't do it to her."

"What are you asking me to do about it?" the judge said.

"I'm asking if I can have the weekend. It's already closing in on the lunch hour. Don't know if you've been paying attention to the forecast, but we're in for about six inches of snowfall in the next two hours. That's gonna make it difficult for a lot of these people to get home this afternoon. I'm asking if you and Ms. Leary wouldn't mind adjourning until Monday, now."

"Monday is December 21st, Mr. Braunlin," the judge reminded him. "Ms. Leary, how many days do you think it's gonna take you to present your defense? I don't want to get into a situation where we're asking these folks to deliberate during Christmas. Then we've got rebuttal to leave time for."

"I will probably need a day, day and a half at most," I said.

"Well, that puts us right up against it, doesn't it?"

"Your Honor, my client is fighting for the rest of his life. As much as I don't want to inconvenience the jury or this court, I'm afraid that just isn't my biggest concern right now. This is going to take as long as it takes."

Judge Homer raised a brow, apparently unimpressed with my argument.

"Here's what we're gonna do. I'm gonna adjourn for the weekend. Mr. Braunlin's right about the weather. The salt trucks and plows won't even get out there until the evening. But

Monday morning, if you don't have your witness ready to go, Lucky, then you're gonna turn this case over to Ms. Leary anyway. Got it?"

Lucky nodded. He hesitated a moment after the judge waved us off. As if he had another point to make but decided against making it.

Instead, Lucky walked up to the lectern. I took my place beside Nick.

"Your Honor," Lucky said. "At this time, the prosecution rests."

I kept a poker face. He was resting? Skipping Trudy's testimony altogether? She could deliver some of his most powerful emotional testimony. Why, I wondered.

"All right then," the judge said. "We're adjourned until Monday, at which time Ms. Leary will call her first witness for the defense. Get home safe, everybody. Weather man says we're in for a wallop."

With that, he banged his gavel.

Chapter 18

"You're amazing. You didn't have to do this."

I could barely see Jeanie's face. She wore a pink knit hat, a matching scarf wound tightly around her mouth and nose so only her eyes peeked out. Her voice was muffled, but she talked loud enough, I could still understand her. She held her phone out using the back camera so I could see both her and the sign on the store behind her.

"Jingle's Christmas Notions. Established 1987."

"Somebody's got to bail you out, kid," Jeanie said.

"But we could have done this over the phone."

Jeanie shook her phone, giving me a headache as I watched through my own phone screen, propping it up against some books so I had a free hand to take notes. Jeanie'd only given me a five-minute warning that she'd be FaceTiming me. I just hoped the call wouldn't drop. I got one bar out here at Dharma and Rich's guest house.

"He's expecting me, come on," Jeanie said. The picture bobbed up and down as Jeanie made her way into the store. For a few moments, I saw nothing but the tops of her green snow boots as she introduced herself to the store owner. Finally, Jeanie's picture stabilized. She appeared to have me propped up on a counter. She adjusted the angle so I could see racks of costumes. Santa Claus, Mrs. Claus, elves, reindeer, snowmen, and a few other red and green offerings I couldn't make out. An older man came into view. Bald with gold wire-framed glasses. He wore a red-and-white-pin-striped dress shirt with the sleeves rolled up and a green apron over it.

"This is Walt," Jeanie said. "Walt Jingle."

"You can't be serious," I muttered.

"Jankowicz originally," the man said. "But I changed it legally a while back. For marketing purposes."

"Well, Mr. Jangle …"

"Jingle," Jeanie corrected.

"Jingle," I said. "Sorry. I really appreciate you taking the time to talk with me. Especially under these rather, um, unusual circumstances."

"Your gal here said you're helping Nick Whittaker out. That's all I needed to know. He's a good one. One of my best customers."

"Tell Cass what you told me," Jeanie said.

"I said it. Nick's one of my best customers."

"No, the bit about the costumes. Better yet. Let's show her."

"Sure thing," Jingle said. He disappeared out of frame.

"He's something, isn't he?" Jeanie whispered, peering down so her face filled the frame. I got a close-up view of the inside of her nostrils.

"Back up," I said. She did, but only a little.

"I wish you were here. This place is like Christmas exploded. He's got candy cane wallpaper. Where do you get candy cane wallpaper? I wish I had smell-o-vision on this thing. The wallpaper smells like peppermint. I am not kidding."

She turned her phone so I could see the back wall of the store. Sure enough, it was covered in green wallpaper with giant candy canes lined up in rows.

"It's a trip," Jeanie said. She put her phone back on the counter just as Jingle walked back out. He was carrying a large red garment bag. He unzipped it and stepped back so I could see what he held. It was the exact Santa suit Nick wore. Thick red velvet trimmed in gold and green.

"This is the Olde World Deluxe," Jingle said. "And this is the display. I just got it back from the dry cleaners. I usually keep it on a mannequin in the store window. Don't sell too many of these."

"Tell her why," Jeanie said.

"The price tag. It's two thousand bucks."

"How many have you sold?" I asked. "Do you have those records?"

"I got 'em somewhere. But Nick's my best customer. I meant that in two ways. Because he's just a good guy. Nice as they come. Dedicated. You know? He brings so much joy when he dresses up. Heck, even when he doesn't. He doesn't have a lot of money. A lot of his appearances, he does pro bono. But every time he comes in he donates to the Children's Hospital down here. And he makes an appearance. Doesn't matter what time of year it is."

"That is nice," I said. "But what's the second reason he's your best customer?"

"Cuz he buys the Olde World Deluxe. Sold him three of these babies in the last five years."

Three, I thought. That's the exact number Detective Haney confiscated from Nick's house the morning after Steve Anspaugh's attack.

"Good, right?" Jeanie said, smiling. She leaned down to put her face in frame again.

"Very good," I said.

"Mr. Jangle ... er ... Jingle ... how detailed are your records on who you sell the Deluxe to?"

"I write out a sales slip. I'm old-fashioned. My kids have been on me to computerize everything. But I like pen and paper. I let them do their spreadsheets and whatnot after the fact. But I've got a file. I'd say I've sold maybe ten of these in the last five years since I started stocking them. It's not my bread and butter."

Walt Jingle disappeared out of frame. A moment later he came back holding a thinner black garment bag. He unzipped it and pulled out another Santa suit. This was a more standard, generic version with a thin plastic belt. I couldn't obviously tell what material it was made out of through Jeanie's phone screen, but it looked like polyester, not velvet.

"These are what I sell the most of. A hundred bucks. Had to up the price last year but they're still going like hotcakes. These are durable. You can throw 'em in the washing machine and dryer and they come out fine. The Olde World Deluxe you gotta either spot clean or send out to the dry cleaners. And even then I don't trust a lot of 'em."

"Ten Olde World Deluxe in five years," I said. "Off the top of your head, besides Nick Whittaker who you said bought three of them, could you find your records on who the other seven customers were?"

"Didn't say there were seven customers. Said there were seven suits. And that's an approximation. I'll have to do some digging."

"Of course. Could you?"

"For Nick? You betcha. I heard what they said he did. Just doesn't track with the guy I know. Though, I suppose you never really know about a person. Can't say I've spent much time with Nick outside of him coming into the store and picking these up. And I've gone with him a few times when he did events here in Frankenmuth. But I've got to special order these suits so he'll tell me when he's ready for a new one."

"Where do you special order them from?"

"Why, the North Pole, of course," Jingle said, shooting me a wink.

"Right. But really. Mr. Jingle, it's important."

"I know that, little lady. I'm just having a little holiday fun. Got to stay in the spirit, you know. And I'm not entirely kidding. These suits are handmade in Reykjavik, Iceland. I'm the only store in North America that sells 'em. Heck, I'm the only place you can get them other than at the source and they don't ship."

"What do you mean they don't ship?"

"I mean you can't just go online and buy the Olde World Deluxe. You either have to trek your way to Reykjavik and pick one up, or you have to trek your way right through my front door and order one."

"So you don't ship either?" I said. "You mean all ten that you've sold, you sold by in-store pickup?"

"Yep. Wouldn't trust any of the parcel delivery services. These are precious cargo."

My wheels spun. Jingle was saying that if my theory was right, Steve Anspaugh's real attacker had been in his store.

"Mr. Jingle, I cannot stress this enough. You've been extremely helpful. The sooner you can get me those sales records, the better. I need names. Addresses, if you've got them. And if you could try to remember a physical description of your buyers. I know that's a lot to ask."

"And now I've said this three times. I'll do anything to try to help Nick Whittaker."

"Good. Because I'm pretty sure I'm going to need you to come to court for him. Do you think you can do that?"

Jingle frowned. He turned and hung the Santa suit back on a rack behind him. "Lady," he said. "It's December 19th. You know what that means, don't you?"

"I do. But I also know that Nick Whittaker is on trial for his freedom. I feel the same way about him that you do. He's a good guy. And I believe he's innocent. I think if you're in the business of spreading the Christmas spirit, there isn't a better way for you to do that than coming to Helene and helping out an old friend."

Jingle slipped his glasses off and squeezed the bridge of his nose. "It could be bad for my business, you know. I just don't mean me not being here a couple of days before Christmas. I mean, it's gonna be a story in the local news."

"I know." I could and would subpoena the man. If I knew Jeanie, she probably already had the paperwork in her pocket.

"All right," Jingle said. "I'll be there with bells on."

I couldn't tell if he was kidding about the bells part. But at this point, I'd take him any way I could get him.

"Hot damn!" Jeanie shouted. She picked up her phone. "You let me know when you've got those sales records. I'm gonna stay in town for a few hours before heading back. I'll wait for your call."

She said a hasty goodbye to Jingle, then walked back out to the parking lot. I had to close my eyes for a second. Her bobbing screen was giving me a headache. She stabilized it and I could see she was now behind the wheel of her car.

"Good work," I said. "This might be the break I need."

"Don't worry. I'm not leaving Frankenmuth until I have copies of that man's sales records. I can sit on him if you want. Drive his Christmas-keister all the way up to Helene on Monday if you want."

"No," I said. "I don't like the idea of you doing all that highway driving, Jeanie."

"Well, I talked to one of his kids. He's got a daughter. She seems pretty sharp. I think I can put her in charge of getting him where he needs to go. They really do like your client around here."

"You're the best."

"Oh, I know. Wrap this up, Cass. We miss you back home."

"I miss you too. I'm doing my best."

"What's next?"

"I'm not sure. Something odd happened in court yesterday. The prosecutor kind of abruptly rested even though he was planning on calling the victim's wife. It would have been a powerful note to end on."

"Jerked-the-heartstrings kind of thing," she said.

"Yes."

"Any idea why?"

"He said something about her being too upset to testify."

"Sounds like that's exactly why he'd want to put her on the stand."

"Yeah."

Jeanie clucked her tongue. "Cass, be careful. I know what you're planning. It's the kind of thing that might backfire if you come in too hot."

"How do you know ..."

"You're gonna go see her, aren't you? The wife."

I smiled. "I'm thinking about it. Yes. So far she's refused my calls. But I just can't shake the feeling there's another reason Lucky Braunlin punted on putting her on the stand. This is a life sentence Nick Whittaker's facing. I can't leave any stones unturned, you know?"

Jeanie shook her head. "Yeah. I know. You just be careful the villagers don't start picking up those stones and throwing them at you."

"I'll be careful," I said. But as usual, I knew she was right. My next visit wasn't going to win me any points with the people of Helene. I just hoped my instincts were right.

Chapter 19

"Are you sure this is a good idea?"

Aimee Whittaker put her car in park. Her windshield wipers made a slow, squeaky swipe, clearing the snow off the glass but leaving a slushy smudge behind.

"I think this is probably a terrible idea," I said. "But I have to try."

"She won't talk to me. We've been friends for thirty years and she won't even look at me if we run into each other. I don't see how it's going to go any easier for you."

"It probably won't," I said, unlatching my seat belt. We sat in the parking lot of a small coffee shop called The Underground. It felt like a pretty subversive name for a quaint little town like Helene. Aimee informed me it was under new ownership, but had been a cafe with a variety of different names for as long as anyone who lived here remembered. None of that was as important as where it was located. Directly across from the Helene County Hospital and Crossroads Nursing Care Center. And every Sunday since July 25th, precisely at two p.m., Trudy Anspaugh had lunch here. She came after spending her morning sitting vigil at her husband's bedside. Aimee knew because she was close friends with one of Steven Anspaugh's day nurses. Aimee Whittaker was close friends with virtually every faction in town. Between her and Dharma Till, I had an invaluable pipeline to town gossip and family histories.

"I should stay in the car," she said. "If Trudy sees me, she might get up and leave."

"Don't be afraid of her. I'm not planning on being aggressive or anything. I'll score no points bullying the victim's wife, Aimee. Even if she's somehow managed to help put an innocent man in prison."

"I'm waiting here. Text me if you need me."

"Got it," I said. I slid the strap of my bag over my shoulder and pulled my coat tighter around me as I stepped out of the car and headed up the walkway.

The Underground was adorable inside. Red leather retro booths, stainless steel stools at the long counter, an old-fashioned cash register that appeared to be working. Trudy Anspaugh sat in the back corner, sipping her coffee and picking the edges of a blueberry muffin.

"Sit anywhere," a waitress called out to me from behind the counter. The place wasn't very busy. We were well past breakfast and even a regular lunch hour. There was only Trudy in the corner, a four-top of young men in scrubs sitting at a booth near the front, and an older couple in the back leaning over a crossword puzzle.

I waved at the waitress and made my way to Trudy's booth, steeling myself for whatever she might say to me.

"Mrs. Anspaugh?" I said. "Do you mind if I sit and talk to you for a moment?" Might as well get right to it. She'd either listen to me, or storm off.

Slowly, she raised her eyes and met mine. I watched as recognition made her smile falter. But she didn't storm off. She didn't say anything. I took that as acquiescence and slid into the empty booth seat across from her.

I reached across the table. "My name is Cass Leary."

"I know who you are. You think I didn't notice you in that courtroom every day?" No real inflection. Not anger. Not sadness. She was just flat.

"Good. Let me just say I'm so sorry for what's happened. For what you're going through. It must be awful. Can you tell me how your husband is doing today? I know you came from the hospital."

"You're spying on me?"

"No. But you haven't returned my calls. I was really hoping you'd be willing to just talk to me for a few minutes."

"What do you want from me?"

Trudy put her muffin down. When the waitress came over to take my order, I smiled and waved her away.

"I'd just like to ask you about what happened. I know everyone in town has already decided that Nick Whittaker's the one who hurt your husband. I'm trying to piece together what happened."

"Hurt. Hurt my husband? I don't know if I think that's a sufficient word for what my husband is. If Steve could say something, I think he'd wish he'd just died that night rather than live ... than exist the way he is right now."

"I can't even imagine. Again, I'm so sorry. And it's not my intention to bring you more distress."

"He's a good man, my Steven. He cares about this community. That's all this ever was."

"This?"

"Christmas lights. Christmas lights! Is that worth a man's life? Or my life? Because he isn't the only victim in this. Sure, Steven's the one lying in that hospital bed needing help to eat. To get dressed. To bathe. But I'm just as much a victim as he is. I didn't sign up for this. I'm forty years old. Steve is supposed to be the one taking care of me, not the other way around."

"Mr. Braunlin was concerned it would be too upsetting for you to take the stand and testify," I said.

"Upset? You bet I'm upset. This is all going to fall on me. All of it. They're not taking care of Steve the way I think they should. Just today, I went up there and he had pudding all down the front of his shirt. They just left him like that."

She lowered her voice at the end, aware of the four gentlemen in scrubs across the restaurant. I found it a little odd. Trudy Anspaugh didn't strike me as fragile today. Braunlin gave me the impression she'd been too hysterical to give her testimony. Again I wondered, why not put her on the stand? She was the one who found her husband. She was the one who could best establish the prosecution's timeline and engender sympathy with the jury. Why not call her?

"Do you have someone helping you?" I asked. "Is your family local? I know that the Anspaughs have been a fixture here since the town was founded. But what about your family?"

"The Anspaughs?" she said, slamming down her napkin. "You think any of them could deal with what I'm dealing with? His mother won't even come visit. My father-in-law? He gives me money so I'm grateful for that. But no, it's just me."

"That must be really hard. You know, there are resources. Support groups. Community programs that ..."

"I'm fine," she snapped.

"You've been through an unbelievable trauma, Mrs. Anspaugh. What you saw that night. What you endured and are enduring. It's too much for one person to handle alone."

"Why are you saying all of this to me? Aren't you the enemy?"

"I am most assuredly not the enemy. I want justice for your husband as much as anyone."

"And you don't think having Nick Whittaker pay for what he did will give us that?"

"Mrs. Anspaugh, do you believe Nick Whittaker could have done this?"

It was a question I could never ask her if she were on the witness stand. Not even Lucky Braunlin would be foolish enough to put the question that way, even over my objections. But here, just the two of us, sitting in this coffee shop, I wanted to read Trudy Anspaugh's face.

Her eyelids fluttered. She blinked away tears. But she didn't give me an answer.

"Surely you must know. Is there anyone else Steve was quarreling with? Anyone you saw him have words with here in town, or who might have come to the house?"

"The police asked me all of this."

"And I've read your statement to them. But that was almost six months ago. You've had more time to process what happened. More time to think. What about Amos Barnett? I'm aware there was bad blood between him and your husband. I had my own run-in with Amos the other day."

"I can't help you," she said, grabbing her purse. She started to scoot out of the booth.

"Can you answer my question? You. Sitting here today. Do you really think in your heart that Nick Whittaker did this to your husband?"

"You should be ashamed of yourself," she said, but had the courtesy to keep her voice down. It seemed she wanted to avoid a scene here at The Underground as much as I did.

"I'm doing my job. Regardless of what you may think, Nick's entitled to a robust defense."

"Do you think he did this to my husband?"

"What?"

"You. Tell me. You've probably seen more than I have. The evidence. The things the cops wouldn't show me. But I know you have. I know they're legally obligated to show you everything. They wouldn't show me. Detective Haney refused my requests every time I went down there to talk to him. The pictures they took. Of my Steven."

"But you saw him yourself," I said. "Why put yourself through it? Reliving it. You were there that night. By his side. Isn't that enough?"

"I have nothing to say to you. If you think Nick's innocent, then prove it. Then we'll talk."

"It doesn't work like that. It's not my job to ..."

She batted her hand at me. "Don't talk to me about justice then. Don't talk to me about Nick Whittaker's rights. What about my rights? My right not to watch my husband wither away and have no choice but to be there by his side. You think he would have done that for me?"

She seemed as if she wanted to say more but stopped herself. Trudy Anspaugh turned on her heel. She stormed out of the restaurant.

"Mrs. Anspaugh?" the waitress called out. "Your bill ..."

"I'll take care of it," I said. I left two twenties on the table and walked up to the waitress.

"Thanks," she said. "It's been tough on her. I know that. She's just getting harder and harder to deal with."

The girl's name tag read "Shaney."

"She comes in every Sunday?" I asked.

Shaney nodded. "She's had a rough go. But that's the third time she's tried to leave without paying."

"She probably just gets distracted," I said. I looked out the front window. Aimee got out of her car. She was looking at something on the far end of the parking lot.

"Does she always come in alone?" I asked Shaney.

"Mostly. She sat with a couple of the nurses for a while. But ... they stopped coming in. Mrs. Anspaugh can be sort of rude. She's just ... I know this is awful to say considering everything going on in her life. But she's a bummer to be around. Just yelling all the time."

"Well, thanks for taking care of her," I said.

"You'll have to come back when you have more time. I'm making our specialty apple pie. It's to die for."

"I'll remember that," I said.

I walked toward the front door, hearing shouting coming from outside. Aimee was still standing outside her vehicle. Two patrons walked in but they were rubbernecking whatever was going on out in the parking lot. I brushed past them and went to Aimee's car.

"How'd it go?" Aimee asked, though she didn't take her eyes off the corner of the lot. I tracked her gaze. There, Trudy Anspaugh stood in front of her car door. She was too far away for me to hear what she was saying, but she had just finished shouting something to the man parked in a pickup beside her. He shouted something back then flipped her off. Then he peeled out of his spot coming close enough to Trudy that she had to dodge to keep from being run over by the truck's back wheel.

"What the hell was that about?" I asked.

Aimee shook her head.

"He just pulled up alongside her. Couldn't hear what they were saying."

The truck zoomed past us on its way out of the lot. I got a clear look at the driver.

"That's ..." I started.

"Amos Barnett," Aimee said.

"He hates her," I said. "I don't know what she said to him, but he looked ready to murder Trudy Anspaugh. I literally just got done asking her about him. She didn't give me an answer. She didn't even acknowledge the question."

For her part, Trudy got behind the wheel of her own car and sped off in the opposite direction.

"I have no idea," Aimee said, getting back in her car. I climbed in beside her. "That man is a menace. He figures out a way to hate everyone in town. I guess it's just Trudy's turn."

Aimee put the car in gear. I pulled out my phone and sent a text to Eric. "You have anything more for me on Amos Barnett or A.J. Barnett yet? I'm running out of time."

Eric texted back as Aimee made the turn to Dover Street heading back to the Tills' guest house.

"I know," he said. "Give me twenty-four more hours. Do you have that long?"

I looked at Aimee. She was trying to keep a brave face, but she looked about ready to cry.

"Barely," I texted back. "It's my case tomorrow morning."

"Who are you putting on?" he asked.

I hesitated before I texted back. Then I sent him a single emoji as my answer. Santa Claus.

Chapter 20

"Do you solemnly swear that the testimony you're about to give will be the truth, the whole truth, and nothing but the truth?"

"Yes. So help me God."

Nick Whittaker cut an imposing figure, towering over the bailiff as he held his right hand up. He wore a crisply pressed black suit with a red tie. Aimee had picked all of it out for him, driving to Petoskey to a Big & Tall men's store. He had his snow-white hair slicked back and his beard neatly trimmed. And still, he looked like Santa Claus.

I stepped up to the lectern and gave Nick an encouraging smile. He folded his hands in his lap and sat up straight, but I could already see a thin trickle of sweat running down his temple and disappearing into his beard.

"Mr. Whittaker," I started. "Can you tell me a little about yourself? How long have you lived in Helene?"

"All my life. I was born here. My parents were born here. My grandparents. Even my great-grandparents. They used to own the apple orchard out on Washington Road. It's changed ownership a few times since then. They sold it before I was born. But the Whittaker Farm was a well-known business for the first half of the twentieth century."

"What about you? Where do you live now?"

"I live in the same house I was born in: 1041 Dover. On the corner of Dover and Hill. My father bought it for my mother right after they got married in 1958. It was brand new then. I lived there with them ... took care of them until they both passed away. I was never going to put either one of them in a home. Even when it got bad. That's just not what Whittakers do."

"Of course," I said. "Mr. Whittaker, what do you do for a living?"

He closed his eyes and let out a breath. "I was an electrician. I guess I still am, though I let my license go. I retired from that full time about twelve years ago. Had a back injury that made it too hard to work. But about twenty-some years ago, I started doing events. I suppose it's obvious who I look like to people."

Nervous laughter filled the courtroom.

"Santa Claus," I said. "Forgive me for stating the obvious, but everything we say here is being recorded by that stenographer sitting in front of you."

"Sure," he said. "Santa Claus. See, I went gray early. Used to be blond but by the time I was, oh, thirty, thirty-two, my hair went totally white. And I'm ... uh ... well, my mother used to say I was big-boned. People have been calling me Mr. Santa for most of my adult life. I finally just embraced it. As soon as I did that, I started getting work. People would actually pay me to come to stuff. Pictures with Santa at the local animal hospital, children's hospitals, parades, store openings. At first, I didn't want to take any money. I just enjoyed doing it. Enjoyed making people happy. Especially the little ones. The believers. But then after my back went out and I couldn't work in my field, well, it just seemed a natural thing to do. And I've loved it. It doesn't feel like work. It's just fun. And to be able to bring such joy to people. Sick kids. Their parents. I gotta be honest, I think I'd go back to doing it for free if I had to."

"I understand," I said. "Mr. Whittaker, playing Santa isn't the only thing you're known for around town though, is it?"

"No, ma'am. Sixteen years ago, I started experimenting with my Christmas lights at the house. This was just after my dad died. My mom was so depressed. That first Christmas, I wanted to do something special. Take her mind off it, you know? So I got this idea to just really go out and construct lighting that would blow her away. She used to like that Chevy Chase movie. The Christmas one where he knocks out the grid with all the lights he strings. It made her laugh. Well, anyway, one thing led to another and by Thanksgiving that year I had the beginnings of what you see at the house today. And I had a friend of mine, a software engineer, come over and help me rig everything so it would light up in time with different Christmas music. Well, the look on my mom's face when we set it up for her the first time. Just ... pure joy."

"That's very sweet," I said. "Have you added to the display?"

"Oh yeah. The sad thing is that it ended up being Mom's last Christmas too. I thought about taking it all down. But see, people started showing up to watch it. I got the idea to make it so other people could enjoy the music part of it too. So now it's hooked up so if you come out there and turn your car radio to 107.2 FM, you can listen along. It's gotten bigger and bigger every year. I've been featured on the news a few times. They wrote an article about me in the *Detroit Free Press* a few years ago. That would have made my folks really happy."

"I'll bet. Mr. Whittaker, your light show has drawn controversy too though, hasn't it?"

"I don't know if you'd call it controversy. Somebody complained. I don't know who. All my neighbors … and see, I don't have that many. But somebody complained and pointed out to the township that I'd need a permit or a variance because of all the traffic my place draws from November through the end of the year. So they told me I'd have to apply for a zoning variance. Which I did. It's still pending. But they told me I could keep the show going until that's decided. So I have. My family goes out there now to make sure it's all going smoothly, so people can enjoy it even though I'm in … since I've been in jail."

He choked up on the last word.

"Mr. Whittaker, can you tell the jury how you know Steven Anspaugh, the victim in this case?"

"I just do. I told you. I've lived in Helene my whole life. So has he. I don't even know when we met for the first time. We just know each other. And he's on the township zoning board. But I knew him … was acquainted with him for years … decades outside of that."

"Are you friends?" I asked.

"Well, we didn't go to lunch, if that's what you mean. We were friendly though. Steve always appreciated me when I'd come to events as Santa. He appreciated how much people love it. He was always very nice. Very complimentary."

"But more recently. He's the person who had the power to put a stop to your light show, wasn't he?"

"I don't believe he was going to do that."

"How do you know? You said he sits on the zoning board. He had a pivotal vote on whether your variance would be granted."

I had to get it out. It's the central question I knew every member of the jury had.

"He would have been pretty influential on it. Yes. But I respected him. I trusted the board would do the right thing. I just don't see how they could shut me down. Everyone loves the light show. They look forward to it. In all the years I've been running it, nobody has told me to stop. I've only ever gotten compliments."

"Mr. Whittaker, I'd like to talk about the night of July 25th. Can you tell me how that day went for you?"

"It was a big day. Everybody heard what Miss Connor had to say. At the library? She started a Christmas in July event there and it kind of snowballed, um ... forgive the pun. Well, a few years ago, she came to me and asked if I'd participate in a bigger way. She asked me to run my lights in July for that week. It's a lot. It takes me about a week to set everything up. Then another week to take it all down. But I was glad to do it. And that night, they asked me to come to the library and do pictures with the kids and hand out presents. I've been doing that for I wanna say six years now. And for free. Miss Connor has tried to pay me but I always donate it right back to the library. You can ask her."

"Thank you. Can you be more specific about your movements that night? What were you doing?"

"I was supposed to be there by six. The event ends at ten but I told her ... and she knows this ... that I have to be out of there around nine. I run the light show later than I would in November because of the sunlight. It has to be pretty much full dark for the light show to be best. Anyway, there were a lot more kids that showed up this year. I'd say it was close to nine thirty before I took a picture with the last one. Then I had to scoot. And it's always tricky. I never want the kids to see me coming and going. Not at events. Not at the house. It kind of spoils the illusion if they see me climbing into my pickup truck instead of a sleigh."

"Naturally. Mr. Whittaker, I'd like to show you what's been marked as Defense Exhibit Nineteen. Do you recognize this photo?"

Nick looked at the picture. "Oh. Yes. That's me at the library event. That's one of the little kids who came. Jenny Flax's little girl. Ivy."

I moved to have the photograph admitted as evidence.

"Mr. Whittaker, is that your natural beard in that photograph?"

He ran his fingers over his long beard. "It is."

"It's not a wig?"

"No, ma'am. I don't wear any wigs with my costume. I don't need to."

"Thank you. So what time did you leave the library event? Do you know precisely?"

"Twenty after nine. I said goodbye to Miss Emily and I went out the service door on the side of the building. I park my truck behind the dumpster out there where nobody can see it. I never go in or out the front doors of the library when I'm in costume."

"Got it. And what did you do after you left?"

"I hightailed it home. The light show was already ongoing. I've got it timed to start at nine during the Christmas in July event. But there's kind of a big deal at ten. I come out the front door and wave during *Jolly Old St. Nicholas*. You know. The song. When it plays the last line, choose for me dear Santa Claus, you will know the best. Pow! Right on best. Out I come and wave."

"Sure."

"And I've got a light sculpture made to look like a sleigh and Rudolph up on the roof. They light up when I come out and Rudolph's nose blinks."

We had a video of the finale. I played it for the jury.

"Mr. Whittaker, on that night, you didn't come out at ten on the dot though, did you? Why not?"

"There was a problem. When I got home, I could see right away some of the lights weren't lighting up. I was getting a fault error on the computer. Rudolph and the sleigh weren't talking to the network."

"What time did you get home?"

"It's a fifteen-minute drive from the library. So nine thirty-five or nine forty. I thought I'd have plenty of time. But then the lights weren't working. There was a glitch."

I played a portion of Russ Garfield's phone video. The time stamp at ten rolled by. I let the jury listen again to Lacey and Gracie Garfield's frustration when Nick didn't appear on cue.

"Did anyone see you coming or going from your house when you pulled in?"

"No. I don't think so. I make it so they can't. I cut my headlights right before I turn into the drive on the side of the house. They're all focused on the front and with the Christmas lights, they just can't see me. I don't want them to."

"So what happened with the glitch?"

"I couldn't figure it out. I ran all my diagnostics. I was starting to panic because I missed the ten p.m. cue. I knew people would get mad out there. They've got little kids. That's awful late for them to be awake, even in the summer."

"What did you do?"

"Well, I finally realized I'd have to go out and check the connections. I keep all the extension cords in the back of the house for this very reason. So nobody can see me fiddling with it while the show's going on. It's dark. Well, it took some time, but I finally found the problem. It was simple. Stupid. But two cords had been pulled apart. Rudy and the sleigh weren't hooked up to the electricity. It really was like that scene from that Chevy Chase movie. I got them reconnected and we were off to the races."

I pressed play on Garfield's video. At ten twenty-seven, Nick could be seen bursting out the front door to a smattering of applause. Rudolph and the sleigh lit up on the roof.

"Ten twenty-seven," I said. "So you're telling us that it took you what, forty-five minutes from the time you came home at twenty minutes to ten until you finally solved your electrical problem?"

"It was a connection problem. But yes. And I'm telling you, those connections were solid when I left for the library. I double checked. I always double check. They can't just miraculously become unhooked."

"What do you mean?"

"I mean somebody had to have gone back there and pulled those two cords apart. Deliberate sabotage."

"Has that ever happened before?"

"Have there been connections that got loose? Sure. But like I said, that's always part of my daily check during the Christmas season. I checked that morning. Everything was fine."

I stepped around the lectern. I squared off with Nick Whittaker.

"Mr. Whittaker, you were seen by several witnesses arguing with Steve Anspaugh on the night of July 25th. Can you explain what happened?"

"Nothing happened," he said, his voice rising. "I ran into him coming out of the bathroom. I knew the vote on my variance was coming up the next week. He asked me how I was doing. I said I was getting antsy to leave because I wanted to be on time at the house. I said something about me hoping I'd be able to keep doing that. I reminded him how much it meant to people. He got angry. Told me it wasn't appropriate for me to put pressure on him about the vote. I wasn't doing that. I didn't mean to do that. But he was the one who was angry. He said he thought better of me than me putting pressure on him or trying to make him feel guilty while I was dressed up as Santa. I wasn't trying to do that. I swear. He caught me off guard, is all. I can't speak to what other people say they saw or heard. I can only tell you that I wasn't angry with him. I was nervous. Sure. I was hopeful that the board would do the right thing. But I wasn't mad at Steve Anspaugh."

I had one last question to ask him. "Mr. Whittaker. Did you attack Steven Anspaugh in the parking lot of the library?"

Nick sat straighter. He leaned forward so his lips nearly pressed against the microphone.

"I did not. I would not. I didn't hurt Steve Anspaugh. I would never hurt him. I never laid a hand on him. It wasn't me. I swear it. I would never do that. I would never hurt somebody like that. Never. No. No. No."

With that, I left Nick Whittaker to Lucky Braunlin.

Chapter 21

"Who's your best friend, Mr. Whittaker?"

Lucky Braunlin took his usual position right at the end of the jury box, leaning against it.

"My best friend?" Nick asked. He looked at me but I kept my expression neutral. If the jury got the impression I was coaching him, we were sunk. It was an innocuous question on the surface, but I knew where this was going.

"Your best friend," Lucky said. "Your lawyer asked you if you and Steve Anspaugh were friends. You said you were more acquaintances, if I recall."

"That's right. We were friendly though."

"I see. So again, I'm asking you. Who in town would you consider your best friend?"

"I have lots of friends."

"Do you go on social outings with them? Dinner? The movies? Hang out at their houses? Who are your best friends, would you say?"

"I go to lots of social events. I don't know why you're asking me that."

"These social events that you go to, isn't it true you go when you're dressed up as Santa Claus, right? I mean, you're not being invited out anywhere as plain old Nick Whittaker, are you?"

"I don't ... that's not ... I don't know."

"You don't have a best friend, do you, Mr. Whittaker?"

"I have lots of friends."

"Your parents had friends. You socialize with your family. But you don't really go out or get invited to places as yourself, as Nick Whittaker, do you?"

"Objection," I said. "We're borderline badgering here, Your Honor."

"Judge, this goes to motive. If the witness could be instructed to answer my question, does he ever get invited out as Nick Whittaker instead of hired to be Santa? That's my question."

"Go ahead and answer, Mr. Whittaker," Judge Homer said.

"I don't know," Nick responded. "I think yes. But if you're going to ask me the last time, I don't remember."

"You don't really have any friends you're not related to, do you, Mr. Whittaker?"

"I don't know."

"In fact, your entire social life ... your entire identity is wrapped up in portraying Santa Claus. That's who you are to the people of Helene, isn't it?"

"It makes them happy and that makes me happy. They call me the Christmas Guy. I like that."

"You like that. It's who you are, isn't it?"

"I like that people call me the Christmas Guy. I like being able to bring people joy and put them in the holiday spirit. What's wrong with that? You're making it sound like there's something wrong with that."

"And in your mind, Steven Anspaugh was in a position to take that away from you, wasn't he?"

"My identity? How can another person take away my identity? No. I don't agree with that."

"You were angry with him though, weren't you? You admitted as much. On the night of July 25th, you confronted Steven Anspaugh in front of witnesses. You were overheard telling him you can't take this away from me. Isn't that right?"

"I don't remember what I said. But like I told Ms. Leary when she asked. Steve was angry with me, not the other way around. He was angry that I brought up the variance vote at the Christmas party. That's all. I wasn't angry with him."

"All right. You testified that nobody saw you coming or going from the library that night. You made sure of that, right?"

"I always make sure of that. I told you. It can spoil the illusion for the little kids if they see me pulling up in my pickup truck. They expect to see me in a sleigh."

"And conveniently, nobody saw you pulling into your driveway after you left the library, despite the fact there were at least thirty cars lined up and watching your house."

"It was dark. I told Ms. Leary. I told the police. I had my driveway built so it curves around the side of the house and into the back, not the front. It's on purpose so nobody can see me pulling up in my pickup truck when the little kids are expecting to see Santa driving a sleigh."

"So we have only your word that you arrived at your house when you said you did."

"I'm telling the truth."

"Ten twenty-seven p.m. That's when you finally appeared in front of your house for your big moment. Your big wave to the crowd."

"I don't remember what time it was. But I can't argue with that man's cell phone video. I knew I was running late. I already said why."

"Rudolph," Lucky said. "You blamed Rudolph for your late arrival. A reindeer is your alibi."

"Objection," I said. "Your Honor, this is badgering."

"I agree. Mr. Braunlin, please try to control yourself, all right?"

"Nobody saw you back there fiddling with your extension cords," Braunlin continued.

"I have no idea if anyone saw me. I was in the back of the house. The cars were all lined up in the front in Pastor Till's parking lot. They wouldn't have been able to see me. They aren't supposed to see me."

"Naturally." Lucky Braunlin left his post at the jury box and stepped back behind the lectern. He paused for a moment while he looked through his notes. It felt like theater. I had every belief the man knew exactly what he meant to ask next.

"You were the only one dressed up as Santa Claus at that library, weren't you?"

"What?"

"You're the only one in town who shows up as Santa Claus at these various events, isn't that right?"

"As far as I know."

"It's your gig. You're it. You're the Christmas Guy."

"Yes."

"You never loaned your costumes out to anyone, have you?"

"No, sir. I wouldn't. They're too expensive. I'd be too afraid something would happen to them."

"Of course. And yet, you've seen the surveillance footage from the front of the library. That's your suit in the video, isn't it?"

"No."

"No?"

"No. Because I never went out the front of the library. So I don't know who that was. I don't know where they got that suit."

"But you can't buy those in town, can you? You special order them, isn't that right?"

"That's right."

"You own three of them."

"Yes."

"And all three were in your possession the night of July 25th. You're not claiming anybody stole your costumes, are you?"

"No. There's the one I was wearing and two more I had in the closet at home. The police took them all."

"You're not claiming any of your suits went missing in the days prior to July 25th, are you?"

"No."

"Good. And nobody else has access to those costumes, do they?"

"What do you mean?"

"I mean, you keep them locked up, don't you?"

"They're in a closet. I keep the house locked. So in that sense, yes, they're locked up."

"Nobody else has access to them. You're not claiming that somebody stole one of your costumes and paraded around with it the night of July 25th, are you?"

"I didn't claim that. I am saying that whoever was in that video at the library, it wasn't me. I didn't do this. I didn't hurt Steve Anspaugh. I didn't. I wouldn't. I haven't. I am innocent."

"Because you would never hurt anyone like that. That's what you said when Ms. Leary was questioning you, didn't you?"

"I didn't do this."

"And you said twice now that you would never hurt anyone like that, isn't that true?"

"I don't know how many times I said it. But it's true."

"Except it's not true, is it, Mr. Whittaker?"

"Asked and answered, Your Honor," I said.

"Judge, I'm permitted to get this witness to recommit to the answer he gave on direct examination and now on cross."

"And you have, Mr. Braunlin, please move on."

"Certainly, Your Honor, I'd be glad to. Mr. Whittaker, when you said you would never hurt anyone like Steve Anspaugh was hurt, that was a lie, wasn't it?"

"It was the truth."

"When you said you never hurt anyone like that, that was a lie, wasn't it?"

"Your Honor," I said.

"Mr. Braunlin, I really hope you have a point with all of this. You've now asked the witness the same question at least three times. And he's answered you."

"All right," Lucky said. "Mr. Whittaker, isn't it true that you in fact have hurt someone much in the way Steve Anspaugh was hurt?"

"What?"

I felt my stomach drop. He had something. Lucky Braunlin was too experienced a lawyer to go this hard without having a reason. Nick looked helplessly at me. There was nothing I could do. Like it or not, this was legitimate cross. If Nick hadn't made the claim that he'd never hurt anyone before, I could argue relevancy. But he had. Dammit. He had.

"Mr. Whittaker, who is Greg Fuller?"

"I don't ... what does that have to do with anything?"

"Who is Greg Fuller? You know him, don't you?"

"We went to high school together. But I haven't seen him since. Not in forty years."

"Were you friends with Greg Fuller?"

"Not especially, no."

"Why weren't you friends?"

"We just weren't. And this is ludicrous. Why are you bringing something up that happened more than forty years ago?"

Lord. No. It was as if Lucky Braunlin's next question formed an actual thought bubble like in a cartoon. I could see it there in my mind, suspended in the air.

"Mr. Whittaker, you weren't friends with Greg Fuller, because you beat him so badly he ended up in the hospital, isn't that true?"

"Objection," I shouted. "Counsel is testifying. I'd ask that his last question be stricken from the record."

"Mr. Braunlin, I agree. The jury will disregard that last question. You can try again, counselor. Do better."

"Of course, Your Honor, my apologies." But it was too late. Far too late. Nick was sweating profusely. A damp spot appeared under his collar. He pulled at his tie.

"Mr. Whittaker, what happened between you and Greg Fuller when you were sixteen years old?"

"I was a kid. You can't ask me about that. I was a kid."

"I most certainly can. Mr. Whittaker, you testified that you would never hurt anyone like Mr. Anspaugh was hurt. And I asked you if that was a lie. Was it?"

"I wasn't lying. I didn't hurt Steve. I wouldn't hurt Steve."

"But you have hurt someone you got angry with, haven't you? You hurt Greg Fuller, didn't you?"

"You have to understand. Greg was a bully. He was bad news. You can ask anyone. We went to high school together but he didn't graduate. Ask anyone. He got expelled because he was a bully. A mean, violent, bully."

"Your Honor," Lucky said. "I'd ask you to admonish the witness for being unresponsive. I asked him a simple question. I asked him if he hurt Greg Fuller."

"Mr. Whittaker, please answer the question."

Nick looked straight at me. He mouthed two words. I'm sorry.

"Your Honor," I said. "To the extent Mr. Braunlin is asking about alleged prior bad acts by the witness, the rules of evidence prohibit it. I can't even ..."

"Judge, again. Mr. Whittaker testified he'd never hurt anyone. I'm entitled to explore that answer. I'm entitled to pursue impeachment."

"He's right, Ms. Leary. The witness must answer."

"Did you hurt Greg Fuller?" Lucky shouted.

"Yes!" Nick shouted back. "I hurt him. I hurt him because he called me names. Because he called Mrs. Adler, our science teacher, a very bad name. One I will not repeat. It went on and on and on. Every day. He called me fat. He called me ugly. He pushed me down. He was a bully. It wasn't just me. He terrorized everyone in that school. He got expelled for it."

"He pushed you. He made you angry, is that what you're telling me?"

"Yes! He made everyone angry. He was a bully."

"He made you so angry, you finally snapped, didn't you? You punched him. You kicked him when he was on the ground. You broke two of his ribs and his nose, didn't you? And you would have kept on kicking when he was on the ground if two teachers hadn't pulled you off of him, isn't that right?"

"You Honor," I said. "Again, counsel is testifying. His entire speech should be stricken."

"Isn't that true, Mr. Whittaker?" Lucky shouted. Judge Homer banged his gavel.

"Yes!" Nick yelled. "Yes! I kicked Greg. He wouldn't stop. He wouldn't shut up. Mrs. Adler was crying. Greg was mean."

"He wouldn't shut up," Lucky said. "So you shut him up."

"Your Honor," I said. "There's an objection outstanding."

"Mr. Braunlin, you can ask the witness to tell you if he knows the extent of Greg Fuller's injuries. You may not testify to them yourself. The jury should ignore that. Proceed."

"How badly did you hurt Greg Fuller?" Lucky asked; now he was sweating too.

"Bad," Nick said through tears. "I hurt him very badly. I didn't mean to. I didn't want to hurt him. But he wouldn't stop. He kept being so mean to Mrs. Adler. To me. To everyone. I'd heard he hurt Kim Dunning. She was a friend of mine. A cheerleader.

She was nice to me. And Greg tried to kiss her when she didn't want him to."

"Did you see him do that?"

"No. But I heard."

"How badly did you hurt Greg Fuller?"

"Like you said. I ... he had some broken bones. But I'm telling you, he was ..."

"He had it coming, is that what you mean to say?"

Nick just shook his head.

"Your Honor," Lucky said. "I have no further questions for this witness."

"Ms. Leary?"

Nick was still crying. I had only one question I could ask. I was angry. Angry at him. Angry at Aimee Whittaker. He should have told me this. None of it meant he was guilty of assaulting Steve Anspaugh, but Lucky Braunlin had just proven that he was capable of it.

"Mr. Whittaker," I said. "Did you attack Steve Anspaugh on the night of July 25th?"

"No," he cried, his voice barely more than a whisper. Then again. Louder. Stronger.

"No."

But the damage was already done.

Chapter 22

"I'm sorry."

I couldn't sit. I couldn't stop wearing a hole into the floor as I paced in front of the table. Nick Whittaker sat with his head in his hands. Two sheriff deputies stood outside the courthouse conference room. We had thirty minutes until the judge called us back in for the afternoon session.

I went to the window. The sky had turned pure white. Fat flakes of snow cascaded down, covering the cars in the lot below in under an hour. The forecast called for blizzard conditions to begin the day after Christmas, four days from now. By then, Nick Whittaker's fate would perhaps already be decided.

"It wasn't a lie," Nick said. "I didn't lie. He kept wanting me to admit that I lied. I didn't hurt Steve Anspaugh. I'm innocent."

"Nick," I said. "You may be innocent. But Lucky Braunlin is going to now argue to the jury that you're capable of violence. That you have a history of resorting to it when pushed. Do you see the problem? Do you see why you should have told me about what happened with Greg Fuller?"

"No," he said. "Cass, I was sixteen years old. It was over forty years ago. I barely even remembered it, much less thought it was relevant to any of this."

The door opened. Aimee Whittaker stepped inside, her expression pained. She went to her cousin.

"It's going to be okay, Nick. Don't worry. It's all going to be okay."

I wished I shared her confidence.

"Did you know?" I asked her, unable to keep the edge out of my tone.

"About Greg Fuller? Of course I knew. Everyone knows."

"Except for me," I said. "Do you see why I have a problem with that?"

"Greg Fuller?" she said as if the name should mean something to me. "Cass, half the town wanted to beat the hell out of Greg Fuller. Probably half that jury, if they remember who he was. Is."

"Who is he?"

"A bully," Nick answered. "An absolute thug."

"He's a criminal," Aimee said. She planted a kiss on Nick's cheek then took the seat beside him. She rubbed his back as he kept his head buried in his hands.

"He's in prison, Cass," Aimee continued. "Last I heard he's down in Jackson. He robbed the liquor store on Ryder Road. Put the owner in the hospital. Before that, he used to beat on his girlfriend. Lola Paulson. She works at the grocery store on Main. Go ask Lola about him if you don't believe me. Have her smile for you and show you her bridge work. Greg threw a frying pan at her once when he didn't like the way she cooked his eggs. Knocked out her four front teeth. He's a bad seed, Cass. Nick's one of the only people who ever stood up to him. Trust me, he was provoked. He didn't just randomly snap one day."

"The point is, Lucky's going to want to argue that when you're pushed. When you perceive yourself to be threatened, you have resorted to violence in the past. Had I known about this, I could have got it out in the open. I could have figured out a way to spin it on your direct examination, at the very least. Or I could have made a different decision about putting you on the stand at all."

"You had to let me tell them," Nick said. "That jury needed to hear me say I didn't do this. They'll believe me. They have to believe me."

"Enough," Aimee said. "I brought you lunch." She picked up a paper bag off the floor. She pulled out a submarine sandwich and a bag of chips for Nick. She offered another sandwich to me but I waved her off. I'd eat after court was done for the day. Right now, I had no appetite.

"I'm sorry," Nick said. "I really am. I never thought that stuff with Greg would even come up. I don't know how Mr. Braunlin knows about it. It happened before he was born."

There was no point arguing with him or Aimee anymore. This particular bell had already been rung.

"You could put Lola on the stand, maybe," Aimee said. "She'll tell the jury how Greg Fuller deserved everything he got."

"I know you mean well, but that won't help. Our best bet is to just move on. I'll clean up what I can in closing. The evidence against you is still weak. And I've got a few tricks up my sleeve. Just stay positive. We've got a lot of trial to go yet."

I turned back toward the window. It seemed like another inch of snow had fallen just in the last few minutes.

"They won't even bother plowing again until this stops," Aimee said. "Judge Homer might want to end early again."

"He wants this wrapped up so the jury can deliberate before the holiday."

I had an incoming text. In this part of the courthouse, I could only get one bar.

It was Eric. "Got a sec for a phone call?" he texted. I checked the time. We had a good twenty minutes before I had to call my next witness.

"I'm going to head downstairs," I told Aimee and Nick. "Reception is better down there. I need to make a quick call. The deputies will be back in a few minutes to take you into the courtroom, Nick."

"I'll stay with him," Aimee said.

"Thanks."

I excused myself and took the stairs to the courthouse lobby. It wasn't very private there, but at least I could get a better signal. I punched in Eric's number.

"Hey, Cass," he answered. "How's it going up there?"

"Shaky. My client neglected to tell me he beat the crap out of a classmate and put him in the hospital when he was a kid. Prosecutor used it to impeach him today."

"Damn. Nothing like that showed up on his record. Even if he was a juvenile, I would have seen it."

"Doesn't appear that any arrest was made. The victim provoked him. This was over forty years ago. I doubt the school would have even called the police for something like that back then. Kids being kids. The victim had threatened a teacher or something."

"So your guy did society a favor?"

"Something like that. It's just a mess I have to figure out how to clean up. I'm running out of time, Eric. Please tell me you're calling with good news."

"Maybe," he said. "I've been trying to build a more detailed profile of this Amos Barnett like you asked. Couldn't find the wife. I tracked her to an address in Novi, but it's not current. Neighbor said she thinks she moved down south somewhere. I can keep trying."

"I'm not sure how helpful she'll be even if you do find her. I appreciate it though, Eric."

"Oh, before I forget. I just sent you an email. Jeanie got the records you wanted from that shopkeeper in Frankenmuth. He's got the sales invoices for three other customers he sold those costumes to in the last five years. I did some checking. Besides your guy, he sold it to somebody in Milwaukee two years ago. Uh ... let me look. Jeanie cc'd me on the email. Yeah. Edward Shallot. He died a year ago. Two other customers. One paid by credit card, the other cash. The credit card guy was Terrence Jefferson on behalf of Wellman Properties. Wellman's the landlord of a strip mall in Fort Wayne, Indiana. They've got a big holiday wonderland exhibit every year. I talked to the store manager. He says they hire a guy by the name of George Digby as their mall Santa every year. I'm trying to track him down. But the store manager says their Santa costumes are kept in a storage unit. Jeanie's working on getting an affidavit from them. You think the judge will admit it?"

"It depends. Walt Jingle is prepared to testify to all of this?"

"Jeanie says yes. He'll bring the originals of all his sales records with him. You're putting him on first thing in the morning?"

"If I make it through today. I don't know. I'd like to wring Nick and Aimee Whittaker's necks on this prior assault."

"Nobody's perfect, Cass. One incident forty years ago doesn't prove he's guilty of this crime."

"I know. I just hate surprises. So who's Jingle's other customer?"

"Unknown," Eric answered. "That's the one who paid cash. You've got the sales invoice in your email. Customer didn't leave an address or contact information. He signed in cursive. Looks like Thomas Oaks, maybe? It's hard to read. Anyway, you've got it in your email and you can ask your storekeeper about it on the stand. The bottom line, there are other costumes out there identical to what Whittaker has. That's your hook in closing. It could have been anybody on that surveillance footage. You've got reasonable doubt on that alone, Cass. I know you. You'll get the jury there."

"Thanks. I just really want an alternative suspect to give them other than a random person in a Santa suit."

"Oh, Barnett," Eric said. "I do have something you might like."

"His criminal record is sparse, you said."

"I told you I struck out finding the wife. But her name turned up in some other records. Turns out there was a report made to children's services two years ago. Someone at Barnett's son's school noticed bruising on the kid's arms. The kind you usually only get when you've been grabbed, you know? Now, this was all sealed, but I pulled some strings with the school resource officer."

"His kid?" I said. "Eric, I told you. A.J. was hanging out by the church the other night. He was watching me."

"Understood. Like I said, the kid's clean so far. Look, nothing came of the report with children's services. They sent a case worker out but he found no evidence of abuse or neglect. Doesn't mean it wasn't happening. But there was nothing actionable. The case was closed. Only that's not the interesting thing."

"Ms. Leary?" a female voice called me. I turned. I recognized the speaker as Judge Homer's office administrator.

"Judge wants you back in fifteen minutes," she said. I held a finger up, acknowledging her.

"Eric, I'm due back in court. What's the interesting thing?"

"The interesting thing is the complainant. These things are supposed to be kept confidential but they rarely are. The parents usually figure out who ratted on them. Anyway, the report was made by a teacher's aide in the kid's classroom. Cass, it was Trudy Anspaugh."

My ears started to ring. I asked Eric to repeat what he'd just said.

"Trudy Anspaugh's the one who went to the SRO. She noticed the bruises on Amos Junior. Cass, if Amos Barnett found out it was her who snitched on him ... and I'd bet my left arm he did ..."

I sank down and sat on the bench against the wall. Trudy Anspaugh. Amos Barnett was shouting at her in the parking lot of the coffee shop the other day. She looked scared of him. Steve Anspaugh had voted against Barnett's housing development.

"Cass?" Eric said. "Did you get all of that? Listen, if you put the school resource officer on the stand, he can testify to all of this, maybe. If you can clear any objection from the prosecutor."

"I'm running out of time," I said. "Eric, thank you. I've got to go."

My pulse raced. I ran up the stairs, taking them two by two.

Trudy Anspaugh reported Amos Barnett for suspected child abuse. Steve Anspaugh denied Barnett's request for a variance, effectively killing his business plans. And A.J. Barnett was lurking around the house I'm staying in. There was something there. There had to be. I just had no earthly clue how I was going to make use of any of it with the time I had left.

"All rise!" I made it into Judge Homer's courtroom just in time. Nick Whittaker was already at the table. His shoulders dropped with relief when he saw me. I looked over at the bench behind the prosecution's table. Trudy Anspaugh was there, staring straight ahead.

"Ms. Leary?" Judge Homer said.

"Your Honor," I said, clearing my throat. "The defense calls Trudy Anspaugh to the stand."

"What?" she said. "You can't ..."

"Mrs. Anspaugh," Judge Homer called out. "Please take your seat in the witness box."

Chapter 23

"Your Honor, I'd like permission to treat this witness as hostile."

Judge Homer eyed me. Trudy Anspaugh froze where she stood in front of the jury box.

"Can she do this?" Trudy asked. "Can she make me testify?"

"Yes, Mrs. Anspaugh," Judge Homer said. "And your motion is granted, Ms. Leary. Mrs. Anspaugh, please take your oath and step into the box."

Trudy did as she was told. Her entire body trembled. I kept my distance, keeping the lectern between us. I'd have to come at her hard in a minute, but if I could put her at ease first, I knew I might get better answers out of her.

"Mrs. Anspaugh, I know this is going to seem obvious, but that court reporter is making a transcript of everything that's being said in court. So I need to ask you, how are you related to the victim in this case, Steven Anspaugh?"

"He's my husband," she said, tight-lipped. "We've been married for eighteen years."

"Thank you. Would you mind telling me how you met?"

She settled a little, just as I hoped. "A friend introduced us. I wasn't born here in Helene. I'm from Midland. But I have an aunt ... er ... had an aunt who lived up here. We'd come up for various holidays. Then my aunt broke her hip and I came to stay with her for a few weeks while she rehabbed it. Her neighbor, the friend I mentioned. She set me up on a blind date with Steve. She happened to be his cousin. We hit it off right away. He was ... Steve was very attractive to me. And he was figured out, you know? He was already working as a fireman. Had his own house. His family was so nice to me. Well, I knew right away he was the one for me. I was just finishing up my teaching degree at Central Michigan. When it came time for me to do my student teaching, there was an opening here at Helene Middle School. I spent that school year up here and by the time spring rolled around, Steve asked me to marry him. The rest is history."

"It sure is," I said, smiling. "Was Steve always on the zoning board?"

"Oh, no. He didn't get into local politics until after ... well ... we tried to have kids for a long time. It just didn't work out. I've got bad eggs. But he said it didn't matter. Anyway ... once we were done trying, he asked if I'd mind if he ran for office. His family is well known here in Helene. His grandfather was the township supervisor way back. But I supported Steve's decision. I always support Steve's decisions. He's been on the zoning board for twelve years now."

"Got it. That has to be hard though."

"What do you mean?"

"Well, I mean, he certainly can't make everyone happy all the time."

"Steve is fair. He's never made a punitive decision while he's sat on that board. He delivers reasoned, well-supported decisions. He doesn't just rubber stamp things or engage in blanket denials when people make requests of the boards."

It was nowhere near an answer to any question I'd asked, but I let it stand for now.

"Mrs. Anspaugh, what about you? What do you do for a living?"

"I'm not working now. I haven't since Steve's accident. I don't know how anyone could expect me to."

"Of course. But before that ..."

"Before that I believe I told you. I was a teacher at Helene Middle School. I did that for a number of years. Around the time Steve ran for office, I scaled back though. My aunt became ill. She moved in with us and I became her primary caregiver. For five years she lived with stage IV breast cancer. I'll never regret the time I spent with her."

"It's very commendable of you. I'm sure you were a great comfort to her and the rest of your family."

"You take care of people you love. That's the pact we make. It's the same with Steve. For better or worse, in sickness and in health."

"Of course. After your aunt passed away, you went back to work at Helene Middle School, didn't you?"

"I went back part time. I worked as a Title I aide. Steve supported that. He was making enough money for the both of us."

"Got it. Mrs. Anspaugh, I need to ask you some difficult questions. I really don't want to upset you or add to the stress you must be under, but it's important."

"You can ask me anything you want. But you might not like the answers I give you, Ms. Leary."

"Fair enough. Mrs. Anspaugh, you said your husband tried to give fair and reasoned rulings in his capacity as a zoning board member, isn't that right?"

"That's what I said and that's the truth. Yes."

"But he made enemies anyway, didn't he?"

"Everyone liked Steve. Most people understood he was just doing his job."

"Most people, but not all people. Isn't it true that your husband voted to deny an important zoning variance to Amos Barnett?"

Trudy's posture changed. Her shoulders tightened. Her lips disappeared into a bloodless line.

"I don't know anything about that."

"You do though. In fact, you've had run-ins with Amos Barnett on several occasions, haven't you? He hasn't been shy about showing his anger toward your husband after his appeal was denied, isn't that right?"

"You'd have to ask Steve," she said. "Oh, that's right. You can't!"

"I'm not talking about Steve specifically. I'm talking about you. You personally. You aren't on friendly terms with Amos Barnett, are you?"

"He's not a nice man," she said. "But it's not my nature to speak ill of people behind their backs, Ms. Leary."

"Isn't it true that Amos Barnett threatened your husband?"

"Again, you'd have to ask Steve about that."

"But he threatened you too, didn't he?"

"Can she ask me about that? She can't ask me about that, can she?" Trudy looked at Judge Homer.

"You may answer the question, Mrs. Anspaugh."

She didn't though. She stared straight ahead then looked at Lucky Braunlin.

"You had heated words with Amos Barnett as recently as last week, didn't you? He approached you in The Underground parking lot not five minutes after you spoke with me. You remember that, don't you?"

"Objection!" Lucky Braunlin leapt to his feet. "Your Honor, there is absolutely nothing relevant about an alleged conversation this witness had with someone nearly six months after Steve Anspaugh's brutal attack. I've sat quietly long enough."

"Judge, I can't believe I even have to make the argument. It is one hundred percent relevant and appropriate for me to inquire about other people who might have had a motive to do Steve Anspaugh harm."

"Objection overruled. Mrs. Anspaugh, please answer the question."

"I spoke with Amos," she said. "I don't recall it being right after speaking with you, but if that's what you remember, I won't deny it."

"He was angry. Livid. Isn't that right?"

"You'd have to ask him."

"Mrs. Anspaugh, would you have me and this jury believe that you and Amos Barnett are on amicable terms?"

"I don't know what you want me to say about that."

"Amos blames your husband for losing tens of thousands, if not hundreds of thousands of dollars, isn't that right?"

"He wanted to put in a mobile home park on the acreage off Mallard Road. My husband and the rest of the zoning board ruled that usage was against the township master plan. They had no choice but to vote against him. I can't climb inside Amos's head."

"To your knowledge, it's your husband and you he's singled out for his rage though, isn't it? He hasn't threatened any other board members, has he?"

"I haven't heard that, no."

"You were questioned by Detective Haney after your husband's attack, weren't you?"

"Of course."

"And he asked you whether your husband had any known enemies. Anyone who had a reason to hurt him, didn't he?"

"I don't remember exactly. I was pretty upset when he interviewed me."

"He interviewed you multiple times though, right?"

"I think so."

"And you never mentioned Amos Barnett?"

"I don't know why I would. It was common knowledge that the board voted to deny Amos's variance."

"Mrs. Anspaugh, is there anything else that's not common knowledge that would have given Amos Barnett a reason to be angry with you or your husband?"

"Objection," Braunlin said. "Amos Barnett isn't on trial here. I think we've gone down Ms. Leary's tangential side street long enough."

"Your Honor, it's within my right to inquire whether this witness gave a full and complete statement to the police in conjunction with the investigation into her husband's attack. That's all I'm doing."

"Sustained. Please answer, Mrs. Anspaugh."

"I don't remember the question."

"Is there anything else, any other incident that you can think of that would have made you or your husband an enemy of Amos Barnett?"

She knew what I was asking. I could see it in her eyes. Just a glance. A flicker. But she looked at Lucky Braunlin. My blood heated.

"Yes," she finally said, but it was a whisper.

"Yes?" I asked.

"Yes."

"Would you please tell me what other reason Amos Barnett would have had to be angry with you or your husband?"

"I can't say it. It's confidential."

"It's not, Mrs. Anspaugh. Not here. Isn't it true that you made a report to social services about Amos Barnett Junior?"

"Yes. Okay? It was my duty to report suspected abuse."

"What kind of abuse?"

"Child abuse. Oh lord. This is going to get blown way out of proportion."

"I think you need to explain what you mean, Mrs. Anspaugh," I said.

"I found bruises on A.J. He got paint on his shirt after art class. I walked him down to the office and got him a clean tee shirt from the lost and found. When he took off his old one, I saw bruising on his arms that I felt was suspicious. I made a report. But nothing came of it. The case was closed."

"But Mr. Barnett was angry with you about that, wasn't he?"

"Yes."

"And this took place before or after your husband voted to deny the variance that would have allowed him to turn a profit on his land?"

"It was just before the vote."

"And Mr. Barnett threatened your husband, didn't he?"

"Yes."

"And he threatened you again last week, didn't he?"

"Amos is a blowhard. All talk. All bark, no bite. I'm not afraid of him."

"Mrs. Anspaugh, you never mentioned your suspicions about Amos Barnett to Detective Haney, did you?"

"Why would I? Nothing came of my complaint. It was investigated. I did my duty and left the rest of it to the professionals. I assumed the detective already knew. The school resource officer, Deputy Brown knew. How is it my job to do their job for them? My husband was in critical condition. Steve was and is my main focus. He wouldn't have liked it if I stirred all that up again."

"Mrs. Anspaugh ..." I hesitated. "Wait. Steve wouldn't have liked it if you stirred things up with Amos Barnett again? Is that your testimony?"

"That's what I said. Steve didn't want any more trouble with Amos. He made that clear. He was ... Steve was afraid of him. But I sure wasn't."

"Steve was afraid of Amos Barnett," I said.

"Yes. He didn't want any more trouble. And I didn't want any more arguments about it."

"Did you argue with Steve about it a lot?"

"It was just a source of tension, that's all I'm saying. Every married couple has their differences."

"You thought Steve was wrong on this though, didn't you?"

"I wanted him to stand up to Amos and anyone else who said things that aren't true about us."

"Who was saying things that weren't true?" My pulse quickened. I'd just broken the cardinal rule of cross-examination. Never ask a question you don't know the answer to. But a dam had broken inside Trudy Anspaugh. I could sense it. Feel it. There was something there. Something I hadn't seen. What was it?

"Steve doesn't like conflict, that's all I'm saying. We just had different styles of dealing with people. When I see something wrong, I say something."

"Like you did with Amos and Amos Junior."

"Absolutely. I knew it was the right thing to do. I prayed on it. Sought counsel on it. It was the right thing to do. I'd rather make a hundred reports that turn into nothing than fail to protect a child in need."

"Mrs. Anspaugh, were you and Steve in marital counseling prior to his attack?"

"What does that have to do with anything?" she said.

"Were you?"

"No marriage is perfect. We had our ups and downs."

"Were you down or up on July 25th?"

"I'm done," she said. "I'm not answering that. You should be ashamed of yourself for even asking."

I knew if I pressed, I risked having the jury turn against me. And I risked letting Trudy Anspaugh say something I couldn't control.

"Thank you, Mrs. Anspaugh. I appreciate your candor. I know you've been through so much. You have my sympathy. I'm so sorry all of this has happened to you. I have no further questions."

"Mr. Braunlin."

Lucky Braunlin shot to his feet. The man looked as though he had literal steam coming from his ears. Then he did something that I didn't expect.

"Your Honor," he said. "I think this witness has been through quite enough today. I have no questions for her."

"All right. We'll adjourn until tomorrow morning. Ms. Leary, are you expecting to be able to rest?"

I couldn't take my eyes off Lucky Braunlin. Had he known about Trudy's report to social services on Amos Barnett? Is that why he changed his mind and hadn't put her on the stand during his case in chief? Was there something else he didn't want me to uncover and that's why he declined to cross-examine her?

I was missing something. I could feel it. And yet I couldn't for the life of me figure out what it was.

"Ms. Leary? Do you anticipate you'll be able to wrap up your defense tomorrow?" the judge asked again.

"I hope so," I said, then gathered my things and started to leave the courtroom. It seemed like half the town had shown up in the spectator gallery today. Dharma Till caught my eye. Trudy had made her way to Pastor Rich. She was in tears now. He put a comforting arm around her. I motioned for Dharma to follow me out into the hall.

"Did you know?" I asked her, keeping my voice low.

"What do you mean?"

"Did the whole town know Trudy Anspaugh thought Amos Barnett was beating his kid?"

"I don't know."

"Did you?"

She lifted her palms. "I didn't."

"What counsel did she get? She said she prayed on it. Were they coming to your husband, Steve and Trudy? Was Amos Junior? Dharma, why was that kid out in the parking lot that night? Was he looking for you or for me?"

"Cass, certain things have to stay sacrosanct."

As she said it, the deputies led Nick Whittaker out of the courtroom in handcuffs. Dharma's expression became pained.

"I need to know what you know," I said.

"You do. I swear."

Trudy came out of the courtroom, her eyes swollen from crying. She stormed past me and went for the stairs. Rich came out behind her and went to Dharma's side.

"She'll be all right," he said. "She's strong. Cass, please don't beat yourself up. We all know you did what you had to do in there."

Dharma slipped her arms around her husband's waist. I wanted to throttle the pair of them.

Chapter 24

WALT JINGLE CAME DRESSED for the part as I called him to the stand first thing Tuesday morning. He wore a sharp, black suit with a red-and-green-striped tie. I hadn't noticed it during our FaceTime call the other day, but his ears stuck out and were squared off at the tips. It gave him an elven appearance that I didn't think was lost on the jury.

"Mr. Jangle," I said.

"Jingle," he corrected me.

"I'm so sorry. Jingle. Just so we're clear, that is your legal name, isn't it?"

"Yes, ma'am. Family name was Jankowicz but I changed it a while back. Helps with my branding."

"Of course."

I took Jingle through his background. How he'd opened a Christmas costume and decoration shop in Frankenmuth after retiring as a tool and die maker.

"Mr. Jingle, does your store have a particular specialty?"

"We sell a whole lot of costumes. Santa. Mrs. Claus. Elves. All sorts. We've got the more traditional-looking offerings. You know, like what you see on Christmas cards and such. And we've branched into some racier stuff. Short skirts, that kind of thing. Those are getting pretty popular. We do pet costumes too. You'd be surprised how many people like dressing their dogs and cats up as reindeer."

"Do you rent costumes or only sell them outright?"

"Both. But sales are my bread and butter. We also sell ornaments, yard decorations, I've got a few Christmas trees in stock too."

"And you're open all year round?"

"It's Frankenmuth, people expect it."

"Mr. Jang ... er ... Jingle. Are you acquainted with the defendant in this case, Nick Whittaker?"

"Sure am. Great fellow."

"Will you tell the jury how you came to make his acquaintance?"

"As a customer. He came in some years back looking to buy Santa costumes. I've been outfitting him for years now."

"What does he buy from you?"

"He gets the Olde World Deluxe Santa costume. It's got all the bells and whistles. Real velvet. Silk lining. Handmade in Reykjavik, Iceland."

I referred to one of Nick's costumes already admitted into evidence. The clerk had arranged for a garment rack to be brought in. I turned it toward the jury and unzipped the black garment bag and rolled the rack right in front of the jury box. During deliberations, they'd have a chance to touch it, even try it on perhaps.

"Do you sell many of the Olde World Deluxe Santa costumes?"

"No, ma'am. I wouldn't say so. That model costs almost two thousand dollars. Only serious performers will shell out for it. Most people want the standard issue, polyester costume. You can throw those in the washer and dryer. This one has to be dry cleaned."

"Do you keep records on how many of the Olde World Deluxe costumes you've sold?"

"I sure do. As I said, I don't sell too many of them. Nick ... Mr. Whittaker is one of my best customers on that score. I've sold him three in the last five years."

"I'd like to mark Defense Exhibit Eight for identification." One by one, I had Jingle authenticate his sales records to Nick Whittaker.

"What all comes with the Deluxe model, Mr. Jingle?"

"The jacket and pants, the leather belt, the hat, white gloves, beard wig. I sell the boots separate."

"In looking at your invoices to Mr. Whittaker, I see a notation regarding the beard wig. Can you explain what that says?"

"Nick doesn't take the beard. I mean, look at him. He doesn't need it. He gives it back to me and tells me to donate it. So I have."

"To be clear, you're saying Nick Whittaker doesn't use the beard wig that comes with this costume?"

"Nope. Er. No. He does not."

"Thank you. Is Nick Whittaker the only customer you've had in the last five years to purchase the Olde World Deluxe Santa costume?"

"No, ma'am. I've sold it to three other customers since I began stocking it."

"Before we get to that. Are you aware of any other stores that sell this particular costume?"

"Only where it's made in Reykjavik. I'm the only authorized seller here in the U.S. So you'd have to either travel to Iceland or get it from me."

"Do you ship them?"

"I do not. I only sell them in the store."

"So the other three customers physically came into your store to purchase these costumes."

"Yes, ma'am."

I introduced the remaining sales invoices Jingle brought with him. Two of them paid by credit card. The Terrence Jefferson of Wellman Properties in Fort Wayne and Edward Shallot from Milwaukee who was now deceased. The final invoice was the customer who paid in cash.

"With regard to your customer, Terrence Jefferson. Do you know how that costume is being used?"

"They have a guy at one of the strip malls in Fort Wayne who dresses up for pictures with kids every year."

"Do you know who they hire for that?"

"No."

"Do you know if it's the same person every year?"

"No."

"And likewise, you have no idea if they still have possession of the costume you sold?"

"I don't know."

"And what about Edward Shallot? Do you know if that suit is still in possession of that customer?"

"I knew you were going to ask me that. I tried to get a hold of Mr. Shallot. His wife told me he's deceased. His suit was donated to their local Salvation Army last year. I couldn't tell you what they did with it. I don't really keep track of what happens to the costumes after they leave my shop."

"Finally, this fourth customer. He paid in cash. Is that typical?"

"Oh no. I don't generally have people coming in and peeling off almost two grand in twenty-dollar bills, ma'am."

"I see. And when did that sale take place?"

"This summer. Guy came on July 10th."

"Do you remember the name of that customer?"

"He wrote down Thomas Oakley."

"Thomas Oakley. Did Mr. Oakley tell you where he was from?"

"Don't remember that. No."

"Did he tell you how he intended to use this costume?"

"No. I don't recall that. I don't recall much about him, to be honest. He was kind of abrupt when he came in. Didn't want to shop around. Just said he wanted to buy the Olde World Deluxe in Double X."

"And that's the same size you've sold to Mr. Whittaker?"

"Yes. And to Mr. Shallot. Only Terrence Jefferson got it in a different size. A large."

"So you're saying this Mr. Oakley came into the shop with the specific and singular purpose of purchasing the Olde World Deluxe Santa suit in size 2X."

"Yes, ma'am."

"Objection," Braunlin said. "That answer calls for speculation. This witness can't competently testify as to what this mystery man's intentions were on the day."

"Well, I believe he just testified the man told him his intentions," Judge Homer said. "Your objection is overruled. Please continue, Ms. Leary."

"I just have a couple more questions, Your Honor," I said. "Mr. Jingle, is there any way someone would know these costumes came from your shop other than word of mouth?"

"Well, I've got a website. My daughter set that up. But all of my costumes have a label sewn into them on the inside. May I?"

Jingle reached for the costume on the rack. He peeled the coat back, revealing a white label with gold lettering sewn into the seam.

"What are you showing me?" I asked. "For the transcript."

"This is my store label. My wife sews these into every costume on the floor. It's got our address, phone number, and the website."

"Thank you. Mr. Jingle, I have one more question. Were you ever contacted by a Detective Mark Haney from the Helene County Sheriff's Department regarding this case?"

"No."

"He never called you."

"No."

"Never stopped by the store to ask you the questions I've just asked you."

"No."

"Were you ever contacted by Mr. Braunlin, the prosecutor in this case? That man sitting over at that table?"

"No, ma'am. I don't know him."

"You're saying no one but me has ever asked you about this costume or who else you've sold it to in the last few years?"

"Nobody other than you and your partner, Ms. Mills. I really like her. She's a firecracker."

"I'll be sure and let her know. She'd like that. Thank you, Mr. Jingle. I have no further questions."

As I turned to walk back to my table, Aimee Whittaker had a huge smile on her face. Nick looked hopeful, but kept his expression far more subdued.

Walt Jingle was a good witness. But we were far from a home run.

"Your witness, Mr. Braunlin," the judge said.

Chapter 25

"THANK you for making the trek down here, Mr. Jangle," Braunlin started.

"You're welcome. And it's still Jingle."

"Oh. Of course. My apologies. Mr. Jingle."

Braunlin tapped his fingers on the side of the lectern, considering his next question. Beside me, Nick wrote a note.

"We're winning now, aren't we?"

I put a hand over his. I wrote simply, "There's still a lot of trial left."

My pen ran dry. I opened my leather portfolio and grabbed a new pen. Three pieces of paper fluttered to the floor. As unobtrusively as I could, I leaned down to pick them up and set them on top of the portfolio.

"Mr. Jingle, how long have you known Nick Whittaker?" Braunlin asked.

"Oh, a while. I'd say ten years almost? I about fell over the first time he walked into my shop."

"Why's that?"

"Well, look at him. I didn't think he could be for real. I've never seen a person look more like a real live Santa Claus in my life. And I've seen a lot. More than most."

"I can imagine. You told Ms. Leary that Nick Whittaker is an acquaintance of yours."

"Yes."

"But that's not how you'd describe him to other people, is it?"

"What do you mean?"

"I mean ... Nick's been coming to your shop for years. Spending quite a bit of money buying that fancy Santa suit. Would you consider him more than just a customer?"

"I'd say."

"A friend?"

"Oh yes. I'd call Nick a friend. He always gets a hold of me whenever he's in the area. I've recommended him lots of times for different events around the state. I'd say he's one of the best Santa performers there is. He ought to be in the Macy's Parade, if you ask me."

"You like Nick?"

"Of course. Everyone likes Nick. How could you not?"

"He knows your family?"

"Well, sure."

"And you'd hate to see anything bad happen to Nick, isn't that right?"

What's he trying to do? Nick wrote.

Trying to show that Jingle is biased. Don't worry about it, I wrote back.

I moved the papers I'd picked up off the floor. One was my copy of Jingle's invoices on the Santa suit. Another was a note from Jeanie with Jingle's cell phone number. The third was the check the Tills wrote me. I hadn't had a chance to cash it yet. I tried to cover it up. I'd not yet told Nick about it. He saw it anyway. Before I could stop him, Nick flipped the check over. His eyes misted with tears when he read the amount.

"You count Nick Whittaker among your friends, is that right?" Braunlin asked.

"Your Honor," I said. "This question has been asked and answered. Repeatedly."

"Let's move on, Mr. Braunlin," the judge said.

"Gladly. Mr. Jingle, you testified that the wigs come with the Deluxe you sold to Nick Whittaker, isn't that true?"

"They come with it. They're included in the price. Yes."

"And these invoices you filled out for Mr. Whittaker, I see here the beard is part of the sale items listed."

"That's standard. But like I said, Nick didn't use the wigs."

"He donated them back to you, that's what you said?"

"Yes, sir."

"Every time?"

"What do you mean?"

"Well, I mean you just testified that you sold three of these suits to Nick Whittaker. Are you saying you're one hundred percent sure Nick never walked out of your store with one of the beards?"

"I guess I don't know what you mean. Nick doesn't use the beard when he dresses up. I've seen him. Lots of times, actually. He's done some events at my store. And he's done some events in Frankenmuth. I recommended him."

"Of course." Braunlin looked like he was going to ask something, but changed his mind. He started tapping his fingers again. Where was he headed?

I looked through my copies of the invoices again. All of them listed the beards as part of the sale. Lucky was right about that. But Jingle's testimony was strong so far.

"So you've seen Nick in costume. Your costume. The ones you've sold him."

"Yes, sir. He's amazing."

"Most definitely. Now ... on these invoices. I see one dated three years ago. That's not your signature on it, is it? It looks like a woman's name."

"Jessica," he said. "That's my daughter. She works with me."

"So on this date, three years ago, your daughter is actually the one who completed the sale of the Santa costume to Nick Whittaker, is that right?"

"I guess so. That's her signature."

"So you can't say for sure whether the beard left the store with Nick that day, can you?"

I stared at the invoices. It was minor, but Braunlin was making a point. I looked again at the Thomas Oakley invoice just to make sure Jingle himself was the one who signed it.

He was. I stared at the buyer's signature again. Thomas Oakley. The man had big, sprawling loops for letters. The "T" in Thomas had a particular flourish. The top of it wasn't connected to the stalk of the letter. It floated in mid-air, with a curly cue on one end.

It was familiar. Unique. I felt the blood rush from my head.

"Mr. Jingle, just to be clear. You said you've seen Nick Whittaker in costume as Santa. Many times, right?"

"Yes, sir."

"So you'd recognize him in costume, right?"

"Well, I suppose. Yes."

"I'd like to direct your attention to the monitor in the corner here. Would you mind watching something for me?"

"Objection," I said, though I could barely hear my own voice through the ringing in my ears. I couldn't take my eyes off the T in Thomas Oakley.

"Ms. Leary?" the judge said. I realized I'd made an objection but had yet to state my grounds for it.

"The question I believe Mr. Braunlin is going to ask calls for speculation."

"I'm going to ask this witness if he recognizes the man on this surveillance footage," Braunlin said. "Mr. Jingle has just testified that he's familiar with Mr. Whittaker. Has seen him in costume on multiple occasions."

"I'll allow it," the judge said.

I looked desperately behind me. Aimee Whittaker read something on my expression. She frowned. I scanned the gallery. Like before, half the town had shown up today. But I felt a particular pair of eyes boring into me. They belonged to Amos Barnett Junior. He sat along the back wall. I hadn't noticed him there before. Had he heard Trudy's testimony? I searched for his father. Amos Senior didn't appear to be here. And there was someone else missing. Someone who had been here almost every day of the trial so far.

As Lucky Braunlin cued the surveillance tape from the library, I grabbed my pen and wrote a hasty note on a scrap of paper. I handed it to Aimee.

She read it and met my eyes; confusion clouded hers. I nodded, making sure she understood.

She crumpled the note and nodded back at me slowly. "Go," I mouthed. "Right now."

"Mr. Jingle, do you recognize the men in this video?"

"Well, I can't say for sure who that one fella is. But that sure looks like Nick. Yeah. That's Nick. Walking out to the woods with the other fella."

"Thank you, Mr. Jingle. I have no further questions."

Sweat poured down my back. It got hard to breathe. I was wrong. I had to be wrong. And yet, as I stood there with every eye in the courtroom on me, I knew I had it right. I just didn't yet know why.

"Mr. Jingle. Do you recognize the man in that video, or just the costume?"

"Can you play it again?" he asked.

I tried to cover for my trembling hands as I walked over to the lectern and pressed the play button.

Time. I needed to stall. I looked behind me, waiting for Aimee Whittaker to reappear. Praying that the person I'd just sent her out to find was still nearby.

I paused the playback. "I'll repeat the question," I said. "Do you recognize the man or the costume?"

"Well, it's kinda tough to see his face. That's my Olde World Deluxe costume for sure. No question about it. It sure looks like Nick though. He walks like that. Kinda lumbers. I suppose wearing the suit with those heavy boots doesn't help."

"Mr. Jingle, when you sold the Olde World Deluxe to Thomas Oakley, you sold the boots to him as well, didn't you?"

"I'd have to check the invoice." He did. "Yep. Boots too."

"What did Thomas Oakley look like? Can you describe him?"

"He was tall. Taller than me. Though that's not saying much. I'm five foot five. He was probably six feet. Maybe six foot one. Medium build. You know, that's what I remember. I remember thinking the Double X was gonna be too big on him if he was buying it for himself. I told him that. Told him he was gonna have to use some extra padding or the jacket was gonna be too roomy for him. He kept on saying he knew what size he wanted."

"What else do you remember about his appearance?" I asked.

"Brown hair. Thick head of it. Kinda had a big nose on him. Bushy eyebrows."

I heard the door open behind me. I wanted a drink of water. I was afraid the whole courtroom would see my hands shake if I picked up my glass. Slowly, I turned. Aimee Whittaker walked back in. Two people came with her. I scanned the back wall again. Amos Junior wasn't there anymore.

I took a breath and turned back to Walt Jingle.

"Mr. Jingle," I said. "If you saw this man again, would you recognize him?"

"I think so," he said. From the corner of my eye, I saw Aimee scoot back into one of the pews. Her companions came with her.

"Yeah," Jingle said. "I'm pretty good with faces."

I turned to the side. Rich and Dharma Till were still making their way down the bench.

"Mr. Jingle," I said. "Do you see the man you knew as Thomas Oakley anywhere in this courtroom?"

I looked down at my copy of the Oakley invoice. The T with the unique flourish. I'd laid it side by side with the check Richard Till had written me. The donation to Nick Whittaker's defense fund on behalf of his small congregation. The T in Till had the exact same flourish as the T in Thomas Oakley.

"Well, I'll be damned," Jingle said. "Sure do. He's right there. That's him. That's Mr. Oakley. Hey, there, Mr. Oakley. Small world!"

Richard Till froze.

I turned and grabbed the deputy sitting behind me and whispered into his ear. He gave me a stern look, but nodded. He rose and went to the back of the courtroom.

I turned to the judge. "Your Honor, I have no further questions."

"Any recross, Mr. Braunlin?" Homer said.

Braunlin gave me a dirty look. He made a great show of rolling his eyes as he headed up to the lectern.

"Mr. Jingle, you testified Nick Whittaker is your friend, right?"

"Objection," I said, sweating. "Asked and answered. Mr. Braunlin is required to confine his recross to the scope of redirect."

Braunlin flapped his hands in frustration, but the judge sided with me.

"Fine," Braunlin said. "Just to reiterate, you identified the man in that video as Nick Whittaker, did you not?"

"I said it looks like Nick. Yep. But ... if somebody else was wearing that same suit ... like Mr. Oakley there. It sure coulda been him too."

Braunlin's face turned beet red as he realized his error.

"I have no further questions," he said, fuming.

Heart racing, I looked behind me. The deputy I flagged stood stalwart at the back doors, preventing one man from leaving. But the doors opened and Amos Junior walked back in. He took his seat against the back of the wall. Dharma Till got up and started to walk to the back of the courtroom. I turned to the judge.

"Your Honor, I call Richard Till to the stand."

Chapter 26

PASTOR RICHARD TILL kept a smile on his face as he walked up to the witness stand. He said the word God with reverence, looking up toward the heavens as he took his oath. He even went so far as to pull out his own pocket bible, that he clutched to his chest as he took his seat.

"Reverend Till," I said. My head spun as I tried to process what just happened. Walt Jingle was clear. Unflappable. The signatures to my eyes looked far too similar to be a coincidence. Richard Till had purchased the exact same costume Nick Whittaker was known for.

Had he done this? I wanted to take half a day to watch that library surveillance video another hundred times. Could it have been the pastor?

It could have. I knew it. He was roughly the same height as Nick. Thinner, but if he'd padded the suit ... But why?

"You're the pastor of what church, Reverend Till?"

"The Perpetual Hope Ministries."

"Can you explain to the jury where your church is located?"

"On Dover Road at the Hill intersection."

"And how close is your church to Nick Whittaker's home?"

"It's right across the street," he said.

I cued the video of Nick's light show Lucky had already introduced into evidence.

"Reverend," I said. "Where do all the cars park when they come out to watch Mr. Whittaker's light show?" An idea formed in my head. Adrenaline rushed through me. Motive. Opportunity. Everything I noticed when I first saw Nick's house. An anonymous complaint was made to the township. The Tills had been supportive of Nick. But what if ...

"They usually park in the west parking lot."

"Of your church, isn't that right?"

"Yes."

"How long have you been the pastor at Perpetual Hope?"

"My wife and I took the ministry over from Reverend Wendall Wentworth several years ago."

"Several years. And Mr. Whittaker's light show was already well established by then, wasn't it?"

"I don't know what you mean by well established."

"I mean, in a sense, you inherited it, didn't you? You weren't the one who gave people permission to park there and watch, did you? They just ... did it?"

Reverend Till smiled. It was slight, but I could have sworn I saw a flicker in his eyes. Anger, perhaps.

"I can't recall."

"Can you recall if Mr. Whittaker ever asked you for permission to allow people to park in the church lot every night during the holiday season?"

"I don't recall having that conversation with him, no."

"Do you recall whether Reverend Wentworth, your predecessor, warned you about what would happen during the Christmas season?"

"He mentioned something about it. I can't recall specifically."

"Did it come as a surprise to you that first Christmas when Mr. Whittaker put out his lights?"

"It was a surprise to me, yes. I believe I might have heard a rumor or two. My wife and I moved to Helene in the month of August."

"How often does Mr. Whittaker run his light show?"

"What do you mean?"

"I mean ... it's every night, isn't it?"

"During the holiday season, yes."

"If you could clarify, how long is that season?"

"He starts it in November, before Thanksgiving. It runs until New Year's Day."

"So, for almost two months out of the year, plus a week in July, your parking lot is filled with onlookers whose focus is directed toward a gaudy Christmas light show, isn't it?"

"If that's how you choose to describe it, yes."

"How does that make you feel, Mr. Till?"

He set his jaw to the side, considering the question. "Feel?"

"Yes. Feel. I mean, that parking lot is packed from the looks of it." I paused the video.

"It's a popular attraction for folks around town, yes."

"Reverend, how many of those spectators are members of your congregation?" By now, the blood roared in my ears.

"I couldn't say."

"Do any of those spectators come into church to worship?"

There was a subtle change to his color. "Not many," he said.

"Not many. The real answer is none of them, isn't that right?"

"Objection," Lucky said. "Now counsel is testifying."

"Sustained. Try again, Ms. Leary."

"Reverend, have you had trouble building your congregation since you took over the church?"

"It's difficult everywhere. Worship is down."

"People just don't come to church like they used to, is that it?"

"This country is suffering from a crisis of faith, yes."

"And yet, your parking lot is filled to the brim every single night during one of the most sacred times of the year, right?"

"Yes." He said. Now every tiny change in him became far less subtle. His cheeks reddened. His lips pursed. Reverend Till clutched his small bible tightly to his chest.

"They come for the light show. To see Santa Claus. LED reindeer. But they never even bother to turn around and see the steeple, the cross at the top of the church. Am I right?"

"Sadly, most people are more concerned with the commercial and material acts of the holiday. But all are welcome."

"They're welcome. And yet, they don't come to worship. They come to take selfies. To appease their children. I would think that in particular would be hard to take for a man of the cloth like you."

"I do what I can."

"But nobody cares. They want the light show. They want to see Santa so he can hand out presents. They ask Nick Whittaker to come to the township party, but they never asked you, did they?"

"It is a great tragedy, the state of the souls in this township, yes. But as I said. I do what I can."

"And you have no choice but to watch, do you? Every single night. While your pews remain empty. While you scrape by trying to keep the lights on. There it is, in all its glowing materialism. Rudolph on the top of the roof."

"Your Honor, is there a question in there?" Lucky said.

"The question is, Reverend Till, you're forced to watch that light show every single night, aren't you?"

"Yes!" he finally shouted. "And every single lost soul with red and green lights in their eyes."

"It's the devil's work, then, isn't it?"

"Objection!"

"It's certainly not the work of the angels," Till said, his temper rising.

"Reverend Till, you made an anonymous complaint to the township, didn't you?"

"I did no such thing."

"But you were aware that Mr. Whittaker had been forced to file for a zoning variance, isn't that right? Even though he'd had his light show going for over fifteen years."

"I was aware he had some scuttlebutt with the township. But I have nothing to do with that."

"You heard Walt Jingle's testimony, didn't you?"

"Not all of it."

"Mr. Jingle recognized you as having come to his store and purchasing a Santa suit identical to the one Nick Whittaker wears. You heard that, right?"

"I heard him say that. Yes. But Mr. Jingle is mistaken."

I went to my table and picked up the check he'd written me. "Your Honor, I'd like to mark this as Defense Exhibit Eighteen for identification. I regret I haven't had a chance to make copies." I showed the check to Lucky Braunlin. Then I brought it up to the judge. Finally, I handed it to Reverend Till.

"Reverend, do you recognize that document?"

"Of course. It's a check I wrote to you on behalf of my congregation to help defray the costs of your client's legal defense."

"And that's your signature on the check?"

"Yes."

"I'd like to show you what's been marked as Defense Exhibit Seventeen."

I handed him Jingle's sales invoice signed by Thomas Oakley.

From the corner of my eye, I saw realization dawn on Lucky Braunlin's face. He leapt to his feet.

"Objection. If Ms. Leary is planning on asking this witness to compare these documents, he's no expert. He's not qualified."

"I'm not asking him to testify as any kind of expert. I promise, Your Honor, my question will be narrowly confined to what this witness personally observed or did."

"You may proceed."

"Mr. Till," I said. "Do you recognize this document?"

Till's hands shook as he looked at the invoice. "No," he said.

"No? What about the signature at the bottom. Can you read it?"

"It appears to say Thomas Oakley."

"Did you write it?"

"No!"

"Did you frequent Walt Jingle's costume shop in Frankenmuth?"

"No. He's mistaken or he's flat out lying. Or you did this! You did this! You coached that man about what to say. This is nothing more than a cheap stunt because you're desperate. Your client is guilty and you need some sort of scapegoat. Well, I won't play. I have nothing more to say to you."

Till tried to stand up.

"Pastor Till," Judge Homer shouted. "You aren't at liberty to leave the witness stand until you're told."

"She's a liar. The devil is moving through her. I will not take the blame for Nick Whittaker's sins. I'm surrounded by liars and thieves in this courtroom. By the damned."

Judge Homer banged his gavel. Behind me, I heard a strangled cry. A sob. I turned around. Dharma Till had fallen apart. Her face was blotched and purple as her husband railed from the witness stand.

"Reverend Till," I shouted. "Did you tamper with Nick Whittaker's Christmas lights on the night of July 25th?"

"He swore on the bible!" The shout came from the back of the courtroom.

I and every other person in the courtroom turned. A.J. Barnett was on his feet, standing against the back wall and quaking with either fear or rage.

"A.J?" Aimee said.

"Young man," Judge Homer said. "I'm going to have to ask you to be seated and stay quiet. The jury will disregard that outburst."

Reverend Till was on his feet. His face went pure white. "How dare you accuse me of this?"

"Did you tamper with Nick Whittaker's Christmas lights on the evening of July 25th?" I asked.

"I have nothing more to say to you," Till answered.

"Did you assault Steven Anspaugh on the night of July 25th dressed as Santa Claus?"

"I'll pray for you," he said.

"Did you frame Nick Whittaker for your crime by planting that tire iron in his garbage can?"

"No!" he yelled, quaking with rage. "Damn you to hell for even suggesting such a thing."

I stood my ground. "I have no further questions for this witness."

"I sure as hell do," Lucky said, practically plowing me over to get to the lectern.

Chapter 27

I'd NEVER SEEN a cross-examination quite like the one Lucky Braunlin delivered that day. He spent almost two full minutes sputtering and carving a hand through his hair. He walked away from the lectern, then back to it.

I turned to Aimee and handed her a note. Go find A.J. Barnett. Don't let him leave.

Finally, Braunlin asked his first question of Richard Till.

"Reverend Till, did you have anything whatsoever to do with what happened to Steve Anspaugh?"

"I most certainly did not."

"Is Mr. Jingle mistaken about seeing you in his costume shop?"

"He is either mistaken or outright lying, just like I told that lawyer."

So I was "that lawyer" now.

"Isn't it true that you've actually tried to do everything you can to help Nick Whittaker?"

"Yes," he hissed.

"You testified that your congregation numbers are down. I would imagine that also means revenue for the church is down, am I right?"

"Yes."

"And yet, you wrote a two-thousand-dollar check ... money that could have been used to, say, keep the lights on at the church, as Ms. Leary said. And you handed that money over to Ms. Leary for Mr. Whittaker's benefit?"

"That is correct."

"Reverend, have you ever considered charging for parking for those spectators of Nick Whittaker's Christmas light show?"

"Never."

"But you could have, right? I mean, if there are, oh, twenty, thirty cars in the lot every night and if you charged five dollars per car, that would add up, wouldn't it?"

"I've never considered such a thing."

"You were at the library function on July 25th, weren't you?"

"I was. Dharma wanted to go. She likes watching the youngsters meet Santa."

Lucky nodded. He started pacing in front of the lectern again.

"Your Honor, I have no further questions."

"Ms. Leary?" the judge asked.

"No, Your Honor. I'm through with this witness."

"All right then. Are we ready to proceed?"

"Your Honor, I think we need to meet in chambers." I couldn't believe I was the one asking. That Lucky Braunlin seemed willing to proceed as if Walt Jingle and Richard Till hadn't happened. Meanwhile, A.J. Barnett seemed to know something and he was on the loose.

"All right. We'll take a ten-minute recess. Will you be ready to rest your case at that time, Ms. Leary?"

"Uh ... I'd like to meet in chambers, Judge."

"Fine," he said, then stormed off the bench. There was a mad scramble of people out of the gallery and into the hallway. I couldn't see what happened to Aimee, Dharma, or the reverend.

Lucky and I went into Homer's chambers. The judge never even bothered taking off his robe. He sat perched at the edge of his desk.

"Well?" he said to me, spreading his hands out. "What do you want now, Ms. Leary?"

"What do I want? Judge ... Mr. Braunlin ... I can't believe I even have to point this out. You have a witness who positively identified Richard Till as having purchased the exact same costume Nick Whittaker did. The cops never even questioned him. They never bothered to follow up on where Nick's costumes were made. I know you see what I see with regard to that invoice and Richard Till's signature. Lucky, you've got to take this to Haney. You've got to drop the charges against my client. At best, you've got a case built on shoddy police work. At worst, you're about to try to convict the wrong guy. Till was never even questioned by the police."

"He was questioned," Braunlin said. "It's in Haney's report. He just didn't have anything to do with this."

"Ms. Leary," the judge said. "You're of course free to argue all of your points in closing argument."

"I'll move for a mistrial," I said. "Haney's got me out there doing his job for him."

"I won't grant it," Homer said. "Do you have any more witnesses to call, Ms. Leary?"

I couldn't believe what I was hearing.

"You rushed this case to trial," I said to the judge. "You pretty much forced me to try it with a week's prep time. And now, I've introduced exculpatory evidence that should have been discovered by even a halfway good detective. This is absurd. What you're both doing is a gross miscarriage of justice and I think you know it. This is your last trial. You're halfway out the door. But I will not stand by and let my client pay for this."

"I disagree," Judge Homer said. "And I resent your trying to tell me how to do my job. I'm this close to holding you in contempt. You'll show me the proper amount of respect befitting this robe."

"I'd say I am," I shot back.

"You're about to end up in a cell right next to your client, Ms. Leary," he said. "Enough of this. You make your argument to the jury. You don't like the verdict? You appeal. That's how the process is supposed to work. Now if you're done calling witnesses, let's get this over with. We're three days from Christmas and this jury wants to go home. You gonna call anyone on rebuttal, Lucas?"

"No, Judge."

"Fabulous. You should have plenty of time to get your arguments in and the jury can have this case. Let's get back out there and do our jobs."

He made a shooing gesture. The man was cracked in the head. In all my years of practice, I'd never seen a more incompetent judge.

We walked back into the courtroom. Nick gave me an expectant look. "Where's Aimee?" I whispered to him. Nick shrugged. She hadn't come back. I checked my phone. No calls. No texts. No help. And I had a wild card of a judge forcing me to deliver my closing arguments.

I had nothing. No more witnesses I could call. But the jury heard Walt Jingle. Richard Till was a liar. I had to trust they would see through it. Out of time, I rested my case and prayed I'd done enough.

Nick looked despondent. He'd born up well during Lucky's closing. We'd heard it a hundred times. The argument at the library witnessed by the Rapps and Emily Connor. The infamous surveillance footage. The bloody tire iron found in Nick's garbage can.

Then it was my turn. Twelve hours ago, I would have gone through the evidence one by one. Instead, I took a different tack.

"Ladies and gentlemen," I said. "I can't believe I'm standing here. I can't believe that this judge, this prosecutor, and Detective Mark Haney are forcing you to fix their mistakes. But here we are.

"You don't have a positive identification of Nick Whittaker in that videotape. What you have is a costume. That's it. A costume. There's a reason why none of the Santa suits Detective

Haney confiscated had any blood on them. Because none of them were worn in the commission of this crime. It wasn't Nick.

"You heard Walt Jingle. He stood in court, under oath, and identified the man who purchased an identical costume. Richard Till. Richard Till!

"He's the same height as Nick Whittaker. Put a pillow under that suit and he's the same build. He's spent the last few years watching Nick Whittaker's light show. He knows the cues. He knows the timing. He knows where Nick Whittaker keeps his garbage because he can stare at that house every single day.

"Members of the jury, it's not my job to prove to you why Richard Till did what he did. It's the prosecution's job to prove to you that Nick Whittaker committed this crime beyond a reasonable doubt. To be honest, I can't think of a single case I've tried in my twenty-plus-year career that had more doubt than this one. Mark Haney never bothered finding Walt Jingle. He saw a costume on a video and drew a conclusion rather than taking the time to track down other leads. It was easy. It was a phone call. It was his duty. I'm asking you not to make Nick Whittaker, an innocent man, pay the price for Mark Haney's carelessness and Richard Till's lies. I'm asking you to return the only just verdict you can in this case. Nick Whittaker is not guilty. I'm sorry it's fallen to you to fix the mistakes of those duty bound not to make them. But you have to. You must. Thank you."

I gathered my notes and went to sit by my client. By two o'clock, Judge Homer sent the jury into the deliberations to decide Nick Whittaker's fate. Three days before Christmas.

Chapter 28

"But Ms. Leary, how can they do this? How can they still think I did this?"

I had just a few minutes before the deputy took Nick Whittaker back to his holding cell. In the hallway outside the conference room door, I heard chaos starting to build. Nobody yet knew where Dharma Till ran off to. Reverend Till was back though. He shouted something at Lucky Braunlin.

"We're not done fighting, Nick. Not by a long shot okay?" I said.

"Reverend Till," he said. "He was at the library party. I saw him. I talked to him for a couple of minutes. Then I didn't see him again. He knew exactly what time I had to be back at my house that night. Ms. Leary, he's helped me hook up the electrical for the light show before. Last year, he saw me out there getting set up. He came over and helped. Those cords wouldn't have just come undone by themselves. He did this. He has to be the one. He knew what time I left for the library. He could have just walked right across the street and unplugged Rudolph. He knew that was going to make me late for my appearance that night. He knew! Why would he do this? He never once told me he was mad at me about the lights. Not once. And if he was mad enough to hurt somebody, why didn't he hurt me? Why beat up on poor Steve Anspaugh?"

"I don't know, Nick. Not yet. But these are questions Mark Haney should be asking. I'm going to go talk to him. I'm going to demand he reopen the investigation."

"What good is that going to do if that jury says I'm guilty?"

"Nick, there are so many things wrong with the way this investigation and trial was rushed forward. Whatever that jury decides, it's not the end of it, okay?"

"You mean an appeal?"

"At the very least, yes."

His face fell.

"Nick, you can't give up hope. I need you to hang in there."

"I've been in this place for five months. How long will an appeal take?"

"They haven't convicted you yet. Let's go one step at a time. Okay?"

The deputy poked his head in. I didn't know the man other than the brief moments he'd come to gather Nick, but he looked troubled. I wondered how much he'd heard of Walt Jingle and Richard Till's testimonies. I wondered how close he was to Detective Haney.

"You might want to head home, ma'am," the deputy said. "The roads are starting to get pretty slick out there. They're probably going to prepare for a snow emergency. Judge ordered us to bring in food and blankets for the jury. He's going to have them hunker down here if they're still deliberating into the evening."

"I'll be in touch," I said to Nick. What I didn't say? If that jury deliberated for more than an hour it meant in spite of everything, some members of the panel actually still thought Nick Whittaker was guilty.

"Please don't give up on me," Nick said. "I just can't believe ... it's almost Christmas."

I touched his shoulder. Nick gave me a pained look, then rose and left with the deputy. As the hallway door opened, the crowd and commotion had dispersed. I caught a glimpse of Lucky Braunlin with Reverand Till in the elevator just as the doors closed.

I pulled out my cell phone and called Aimee Whittaker. It went straight to voicemail. Where the hell was she?

I gathered my things and headed straight for the sheriff's department one building over. The deputy had been right. Snow was coming down hard now. The cars parked in the street were covered already. I pulled my coat tight and headed up the stone walk into the next building.

The desk sergeant looked up. "Can you tell me where I'll find Mark Haney?"

"Ms. Leary?" the voice came from behind me. Mark Haney stood there, his hair covered in snow. He brushed it off.

"Can we talk somewhere?"

He exchanged a glance with the sergeant, then gestured for me to follow him. He led me into an empty interview room and shut the door.

"You know why I'm here," I said. "You weren't in the courtroom, but I know you've already heard what happened."

"I heard your jury is deliberating."

"You have to question Richard Till. He had motive and opportunity to do Steve Anspaugh harm. My witness sold an identical Santa costume to him two weeks before the library party. You need to get a warrant and search his house for it. Odds are he got rid of it, but you have to check. And find A.J. Barnett. He knows something. He was pretty upset during the reverend's testimony. I caught him lurking around the church grounds the other day. He's involved in this somehow."

"I've completed my investigation. Nobody saw Richard Till arguing with Steve Anspaugh. It was your client they heard threatening him. I've done my job."

"Not very well," I said, fuming. "You have to talk to him. You have to talk to his wife. She ran out of the courtroom during her husband's testimony and now I can't raise her on her cell. Maybe you should try to interview her before her husband gets a hold of her."

"And I don't appreciate you telling me how to do my job, lady. Your client had his day in court. If you're good at your job, you'll get the verdict you want."

"And then what? Best-case scenario, Whittaker's acquitted. Steve Anspaugh's attacker is still out there. I've just handed the clues to you on a silver platter."

"I think I'm done talking about this with you. I think you need to go cool off somewhere and get out of my face."

"This is your fault. Your screw-up. You never bothered to interview Walt Jingle. His name and phone number is sewn inside every one of Nick's costumes that you confiscated. You never even bothered to pick up a phone. That's inexcusable. It's criminal negligence, Detective. He would have told you what he told me and the jury. Here. Look at these!"

I pulled out the quick phone scan copies I'd made of Till's check and Jingle's sales invoice with the Thomas Oakley signature. "I'm not even a handwriting expert and I can see the similarities. The originals are with the jury now. But you have to follow up with this. You and Lucky Braunlin need to get your acts together. Nick Whittaker never even should have been charged, much less taken to trial."

"That's your opinion. I'm not going to sit here and listen ..."

The door opened. The same desk sergeant poked his head in. "I'm sorry, Mark. But you gotta come out here."

I heard yelling out in the lobby. I rose to my feet. It was Aimee Whittaker. And she wasn't alone.

"What the hell's all this now?"

Upon seeing Haney in the room with me, Aimee barged past the sergeant, dragging Dharma Till along with her.

Chapter 29

Five minutes later, Haney forced Aimee and me to wait on a bench in the lobby. He had Dharma in the interview room with the door closed. Beside me, Aimee wouldn't stop crying.

"I trusted them," she said. "I trusted all of them. Even Haney."

She'd been like this since Haney peeled Dharma Till away from her. Hysterical. Not making sense. It had been Dharma who quietly told Detective Haney she'd like to speak with him alone.

"Did you have any luck finding A.J. Barnett?"

"No. He took off. My cousin lives down the street from the Barnetts. I had him go over there but A.J. hasn't come back home either."

"He knows something." I repeated what I'd said to Detective Haney. "I think he wanted to tell me something the other night. He was lurking outside the Tills' guest house. I thought he was there to threaten me like his father had the other day when we went out to that property. But maybe I've got it all wrong."

Maybe he was trying to help me and Richard Till scared him off."

"This has to be enough," she said. "This is a nightmare. They can't still think Nick's guilty."

"Tell me what Dharma said, Aimee."

Aimee dabbed her eyes. "She tried to run away from me. I knew if Pastor Till got a hold of her it was going to be too late. Cass, you couldn't see Dharma's reaction when her husband was on the stand. She started to shake. To cry. Then she got up and ran out. I went after her. Cornered her in the stairwell."

"And?"

"She said ... she kept saying Richard was overreacting. That she never thought he'd go as far as he did. She asked me to forgive her. Cass, then she said Richard had blown everything out of proportion. She kept saying she swore to him there was nothing going on between her and Steve Anspaugh."

I closed my eyes and threw my head back, knocking it against the wall. "She was sleeping with Anspaugh. My God. Of course. Anspaugh held the power to stop Nick's light show. And if he thought Anspaugh and Dharma were a thing ... he'd have a reason to hurt him and cause trouble for Nick."

"She's terrified of him," Aimee said. "I think Till had her lying for him. I don't know if she knew what he was up to that night or not. But she kept crying over and over that Richard had it all wrong about her and Steve."

"He saw them together, is that it?"

The minutes ticked by. Then a full hour as Aimee and I waited. The door to the interview room stayed shut.

"Ladies?" A new desk sergeant came up to us. There'd been a shift change.

"We're not leaving, Larry," Aimee said. "Not until I know what she said to Haney in there."

"Sure," the sergeant said. "Hey, it's not that. I just got a call down from Judge Homer's office. Um. The jury's back. It's still snowing something awful. If you want to head back to the courthouse through our parking garage, you won't get wet."

"Thank you, Larry," Aimee said, her voice catching. I checked the clock. Three hours. The jury had deliberated for three hours.

It shouldn't matter now. No matter what they decided, there was enough evidence to overturn it if they did the wrong thing. But the thought of poor Nick Whittaker having to wait it out if I couldn't get the judge to set bail pending his appeal. He was right. It could take years.

The sergeant led us through the sheriff's garage and into a private elevator reserved for prisoners. We made our way up to the third floor and Judge Homer's courtroom.

Lucky Braunlin was already there. His face looked ghostly white. Richard Till was nowhere to be seen. Did he know where his wife was now?

"Sergeant," I said to the man, then looked closer. His name plate read Larry Spears. "Do you think you could make sure Dharma Till isn't left alone after she's done with Detective Haney?"

Spears glanced at Braunlin. Then he looked back at me and nodded. "I'll make sure she's taken care of." Then, he leaned in close and whispered. "Good luck. Tell Nick ... good luck."

A moment later, a different deputy led Nick to the defense table. He looked even rougher than when I left him a couple of hours ago. Aimee stood resolute behind him.

The judge took the bench and called for the jury to be led back in. They filed in, each of them looking at Nick as they took their places. A good sign. Maybe. But far too many bizarre things had happened since I came to this little town. I wouldn't take anything for granted.

Not yet.

"Ladies and gentlemen, have you reached a verdict in this case?"

The foreman, a sixty-five-year-old retired plumber, nodded. "We have, Judge. It's unanimous."

The bailiff took the verdict form from him and handed it back to the judge. Judge Homer pursed his lips, nodded, then handed the form to his clerk. She smoothed the paper out on her table, cleared her throat, and read it.

"In the matter of the People of the State of Michigan versus Nicholas Whittaker, we, the jury, find the defendant ... not guilty on all charges."

Thank God. Thank. God.

Nick crumpled beside me. That great big man folded his body against my shoulder and wept with relief. A cheer went up in the gallery behind me. I hadn't paid attention, but as I turned, it looked like half the town had quietly filed in. They were here for Nick. For justice.

I squeezed Nick's hand. "It's over. Merry Christmas."

"Can I go home?" Nick asked.

I turned back and looked at the deputy. He leaned in and touched Nick's shoulder. "It'll probably be a few hours. There's paperwork. But I'll personally see to it you get fast-tracked."

Aimee fell apart again. She leapt over the bench and threw herself into Nick's arms. The two of them cried and hugged.

I felt a tap on my shoulder. I turned. A.J. Barnett stood there, looking solemn.

"Ms. Leary," he said. "C-can I talk to you for a second?"

"Of course," I said. "I've been worried about you, A.J."

"Thanks to the jury," Judge Homer said. "You're dismissed. Take it easy getting home. It's brutal out there."

It was. There was a foot of snow on the ground already and more to come. But for now, none of that mattered. It was December 23rd and Nick Whittaker would be coming home for Christmas.

Chapter 30

"'I'm sorry," A.J. said. He said it about a dozen times as I walked with him to the sheriff's department back through the parking garage.

"You were trying to talk to me the other night, weren't you?" I said. "Mr. Till scared you off."

"He was lying on the stand. He said he didn't have one of those Santa costumes. But I saw him with it. At the library party. The night Mr. Anspaugh got hurt. Mrs. Connor asked me if I'd help carry some folding chairs out of one of the storage rooms. When I went back, I saw Santa. I thought it was Mr. Whittaker until he turned around. It was Mr. Till. He was coming out of the storage room. He didn't see me. I didn't ... I didn't know what to do."

"Why didn't you tell the police, A.J.?"

Silent tears fell down his cheeks. "I should have. But my dad doesn't like me talking to the cops."

The boy seemed terrified. "A.J.," I asked. "If you need help. If you don't feel safe ..."

"No," he said. "I'm okay. Really. My dad? It was hard for a really long time after my mom ran off. But he's not drinking anymore. It's been good now. I swear. He was really angry with Mrs. Anspaugh for calling social services. But it was a blessing. It made my dad get clean. I should have thanked her. I wish I'd thanked her."

"There's still time," I said. "And I think she'd like to hear it."

A.J. nodded.

"Honey," I said. "I know you said your dad doesn't like you talking to the cops. But you know you have to tell them what you saw at the library party. You have to tell them about the reverend."

"I know," he said. "I know."

Mark Haney came down the hall. He still had Dharma Till in an interview room. I rose.

"Detective," I said. "This young man has a story to tell I think you need to hear."

Haney took a hard breath. "Yeah. I'll bet he does. You can wait in my office, son. It's going to be a long night."

By eight o'clock that evening, Mark Haney had finally done the right thing. I waited outside his office. He interviewed A.J. Barnett for an hour. Amos showed up at one point, but he didn't interfere. He let his son tell his story. Haney spent nearly three hours interrogating Dharma Till. At the end of it, Haney issued a warrant for Richard Till's arrest. It remained to be seen whether Dharma would face charges in her own right.

When it was all over, Haney came to find me.

"Nick Whittaker will be processed out within the hour," he said. "Then you can take him home."

"Thank you." I took a seat across from his desk. Haney looked haggard now. His hair disheveled. Dark circles rimmed his eyes.

"How much did Dharma Till know?" I asked.

Haney shook his head. "She claims nothing. Not about the assault itself. Says she had no idea he'd gone to Frankenmuth to buy that suit but says she saw the receipt in the trash. Not the suit. She claims she didn't know what it was for. When she asked him, he told her it was decorations he'd bought for the church this year. Her story is, she forgot all about it."

"But she puts him in Frankenmuth too."

"Yeah."

"And A.J. puts Till at the library party in the suit."

"Brave kid," Haney said. "I just wish he'd have felt comfortable coming to me sooner."

"Can I trust that you'll keep an eye on that kid? He says things are good between him and his dad. But I think we both know that wasn't always true."

"I'll look in on them," Haney promised. "A.J.'s gonna be all right. I'll see to it."

"What about Anspaugh? Was he sleeping with Dharma Till?"

Haney heaved a great sigh. "She's not admitting to an affair. She described it as an intense flirtation."

"Intense enough that her husband grew suspicious," I said. "That coupled with Anspaugh's vote on the zoning variance for Nick ..."

"That's the other thing. She's now admitting that Anspaugh gave her and the reverend a heads-up three weeks before the Christmas in July party that he was gonna grant the variance. He came to the church to tell the reverend in person. According to Dharma, she had no idea her husband was angry about the light show. That he's likely the one who filed the complaint."

"Anspaugh knew," I said. "He knew and he never said anything to anybody."

"Probably. Anyway, Dharma says the reverend was furious. Threw Steve out of the church. She went after him. Caught up with him in the parking lot."

"And proceeded to intensely flirt?"

"Something like that."

"You interviewed her," I said. "Before you arrested Nick."

"She didn't tell me any of this," Haney snapped. "Not a word. I'm working with Braunlin to figure out if he wants to file obstruction charges."

"If?" I said. "Detective, an innocent man has sat in jail for five months. And she knew something. This whole time."

"It's in Braunlin's hands now."

After a knock on the door, one of the deputies poked her head in. "Sorry to interrupt. Nick Whittaker's been processed out. They're bringing him up now. He's asking for you, Ms. Leary."

"I think we're done here anyway," I said to Haney.

"Tell him I'm sorry."

I turned to him. "Tell him yourself."

"It was a solid case against him," Haney said.

There was nothing more I could say to him. As I stepped outside, I ran smack into Lucky Braunlin. His face fell when he saw me.

"Don't start," he said.

"Are you kidding me? Between the two of you and Judge Homer, you've nearly ruined a man's life."

Haney got up and slammed his door, leaving me alone in the hallway with Braunlin.

"You gonna tell me you don't make mistakes?"

"Not ones like this. Not ones that could have ... that should have been avoided with some pretty basic detective work. And what about Thomas Gale, Nick's first lawyer?"

"What about him?" Braunlin said, his voice taking an edge.

"Braunlin, if it weren't for the fact that Homer is set to retire in a week it might be worth my time to file a complaint with the Judicial Tenure Commission. And Gale's abandonment of Nick was unethical at best. Malpractice at worst. I have a duty ... you have a duty to report him to the state bar."

"I wish you wouldn't." Nick Whittaker came around the corner. He was dressed simply in a pair of blue jeans and a red-and-black flannel shirt. His thick white hair and beard were combed to shine. His cheeks had color in them again and his eyes twinkled. For the first time since I met him, he seemed ... jolly.

"Tom Gale's a good man," Nick said. "He just needs a little help. He's sick, Ms. Leary. And it's almost Christmas."

"It's your call," I said. "But if you want to pursue something against him, you have my support."

"I don't," he said. "I just want to get home. I've got an appearance to make."

"It's been a long time, Nick," the deputy said. Sergeant Larry Spears came around the corner.

"We've missed you," Spears said. "It's snowing something fierce out there. Why don't you let us drive you home."

"I'd like that," Nick said, smiling. "You gonna run the lights and sirens, Larry?"

"What are you, twelve?" Larry laughed. "Lights. No sirens."

I walked with them back to the parking garage. Nick and I got in the back seat of Spears's cruiser. True to his word, he turned on his blue and red lights as we made our way through town.

I was tired. Exhausted. In the morning, I had a six-hour drive back home if I planned on making it back for Christmas Eve dinner.

More snow had fallen. It looked like it was close to two feet on the ground. But the plows and salt trucks were working. Sergeant Spears managed to fall in line behind one of the Road Commission's plows. He cleared a sludgy path for us all the way through downtown then turned on Dover Street.

That's when it happened. There was no other traffic driving on the road besides Spears's cruiser and the plow truck. But the streets were lined with cars and people. All waving. All flashing their headlights. Honking. Smiling. Holding up signs.

"Take a good look," Spears said. I caught his eyes in his rearview mirror. The man was crying. He rolled down Nick's window.

"Merry Christmas!" people shouted. It seemed all two thousand citizens of Helene had come out to wave Nick Whittaker—their own personal Santa Claus—on home.

The crowds got thicker as we drove past the high school. Up ahead, I could see the blinking colored lights of Nick's house.

"They came!" Nick said. Tears streamed down his face.

"Of course, they came," I said, feeling my throat grow thick with emotion. "They love you."

"Oh shoot," Nick said. "Larry. You gotta pull in the side driveway. If there're kids in the church lot, they're gonna see. We can't have Santa rolling up in a police car."

"I don't think you need to worry," Spears said. "Everyone's just glad you're coming home."

Spears tuned his radio to 107.2 FM. An old Frank Sinatra standard Christmas carol played as Nick's lights blinked in time with it.

"Oh," Nick said. "I'll have just enough time. Wait ... my costume ..."

"Taken care of," Spears said. "Haney released them to Aimee about an hour ago. You should be all set up inside."

As Spears slowed to make the turn into Nick's side driveway, he turned his radio down. There was still music though. Dozens and dozens of people were out of their cars and lined up in front of Nick's house and the church parking lot.

And they were singing *Jingle Bells*.

Aimee met us in the back of the house. She cried as Nick got out of the cruiser and ran into his cousin's arms.

"This is wonderful," I said to Spears. "Did Aimee plan all of this?"

"She didn't have to," Spears said. "Everyone wanted to do it. Nobody wanted to believe Nick was capable of hurting anybody. We're just really glad you made sure the truth came out. Thank you. We owe you a debt, Ms. Leary."

I climbed out of the car. It was a good snow. Not so cold you couldn't stand outside. But the air was crisp and the falling flakes were beautiful, fluffy and large.

Nick disappeared inside the house. Aimee came to me.

"Come on," she said. "The best view is across the street. We have just enough time."

I went with Aimee. The cars parked at the church had their windows rolled down. Once the carollers subsided, everyone turned up their radios. A few minutes later, the familiar melody of *Jolly Old St. Nicholas* heralded Santa Claus's arrival.

I turned and faced the house. The LED sleigh and Rudolph lit up. The reindeer twinkled and danced as everyone sang along. Then, at the glorious crescendo at the end of the song, Santa Claus himself opened the front door and waved to the crowd. He was met with a deafening cheer.

Nick stayed out for two more songs, waving to the crowd. Performing a jolly dance that delighted the children. And me.

Chapter 31

THE NEXT MORNING, Christmas Eve, I packed the last of my bags. I had a final goodbye to say.

Nick kept his lights on well past midnight last night. The people of Helene wanted to be with him. To let him know how much he meant to them. To show Nick Whittaker that he mattered, whether it was Christmas or not.

Richard Till was apprehended at two in the morning trying to get to the Mackinac Bridge. His car spun out on the ice-covered highway. He'd been found with five thousand dollars cash in a duffle bag. Church donations he planned to abscond with. Haney issued an arrest warrant for Dharma Till as well for obstruction of justice. She turned herself in voluntarily.

Nick opened the door, all smiles. I didn't know if he even went to sleep. But his house smelled delicious. He'd made me pancakes and a steaming pot of coffee.

"Thank you," I said. "I've got time for a quick bite before I hit the road."

Aimee came out from the guest room, yawning. She'd gotten a little drunk on eggnog last night and thought the better of driving.

"You aren't going to be able to hit the road," she said. "Haven't you turned on the news?"

"What?"

Nick and Aimee exchanged a look. "They've shut down all the highways north of Mount Pleasant," Nick said. "A full-scale blizzard blew in last night."

"I'm so sorry," Aimee said. "Your family must be expecting you."

"They are," I said. I pulled out my phone and opened my news app. It was just as Aimee had said. The traffic choppers were showing hundreds stuck on I-75 and US 127.

"It's a miracle there haven't been any fatalities yet," Aimee said. "But you're welcome to stay with me. I know it's not the same as family but ..."

"But nothing," Nick said. "If Cass wants to make it home for Christmas ... then she's gonna make it home for Christmas. I can get you out. I can take you in the sleigh."

"What?" I said.

Aimee laughed. "He means the F-350. He calls it the sleigh. Nick, are you sure?"

"I'm sure. It's the least I can do after everything Cass has done for us. I can get us through using the back roads. The sleigh's got a plow and four-wheel drive. Just give me ten minutes to suit up and I'll have you on your way."

"Are you sure?" I asked. "It's your Christmas too. I don't want to impose."

And I didn't. But the thought of not being with my family on Christmas. Of not being back in Delphi.

"Nonsense," Nick said. He was already throwing things in a duffel bag. He brushed past me and opened his garage door. I followed him.

His red truck looked enormous. It had lights on the top and a giant black plow attachment in front. I walked around to the back of it and laughed. Sure enough, Nick's vanity license plate read "SANTASLEIGH."

"You got little ones at your place?" Nick asked. He had two giant black plastic yard bags on the garage floor. He tossed them into the truck.

"Um ... there's my niece and ..."

Smiling, Nick threw a garment bag in the back of the truck.

"Hop in," he said. "The earlier we get on the road the better."

"Be careful," Aimee said. She brought out two travel mugs of coffee and handed them to Nick. Nick took my luggage and threw it in with his garment bag and the yard bags. Then he offered me a hand as I stepped up into the cab.

ALMOST EIGHT HOURS and three hundred miles later, Nick Whittaker delivered on his Christmas Eve promise. He pulled into my lakeside driveway.

It was filled with cars. My entire family had shown up. Like always. It didn't matter if I was home or not.

"You got somewhere I can change?" Nick asked, his eyes twinkling.

"Uh ... yes. Above the garage. See those back steps? There's an apartment up there. You can ..."

"Keep 'em busy," Nick said. He grabbed his garment bag and climbed out of his truck.

Speechless, I got out and walked up to my own front door.

"You open that oven door one more time and you better plan on leaving your head in it!"

I held the front door open with one hand and covered my mouth with the other to stifle a laugh.

My sister Vangie stood with her back to me. She wore one of our mother's aprons. A frilly thing, green and red. I kept it in a closet under the stairs. Vangie wielded a kitchen knife as my youngest brother Matty had a hand on the oven door.

The heavenly scent of a honey-ham filled my nostrils. Freshly baked bread. Candied yams. "I'm just checking to make sure it's done," Matty said. "Don't need you giving us all botulism."

"You don't get botulism from a ham, genius," Vangie said. "Besides, it was cooked already. I'm just warming it up."

I walked fully into the house and quietly shut the door behind me. Nobody noticed me come in. They were too busy in their own, wonderful chaos.

"I'm hungry," Matty said. "Let's get this show on the road."

Something crashed further in the house. My older brother Joe let out a stream of obscenities.

"I told her!" he shouted. "The trunk on this thing is crooked. I knew this was gonna be a problem all damn season."

My Christmas tree listed to one side in the corner by the French doors on the lakeside. A half a dozen glass ornaments had fallen off and shattered on the wood floor.

"Don't walk in here with bare feet!" Tori shouted. She sat on the couch with an Afghan pulled over her legs.

"I'm on it!" my niece Emma shouted. She got up from the other end of the couch. There was a new boyfriend sitting with her. Prior to her getting up, their limbs had been entwined. Emma walked toward the front of the house. She was the first one to see me.

I put a finger to my lips. Her face lit with a wide smile, but she said nothing.

"Dust mop's in the hall closet," I whispered. I gave her a hug as she went by me.

"They're in rare form," she whispered back. "My dad's three sheets to the wind. Jessa's upstairs. Vangie sent her up there to wash off her face. She came down with so much make-up on, Uncle Matty told her she looked like a French whore. I don't get that at all. Why pick on the French?"

"Son of a ..." Matty shouted. He'd just walked into the living room.

"Emma, hurry up with that broom!" Joe shouted. "Your uncle's too much of an idiot not to cut his own damn foot on the glass."

Emma turned back. "I'll bring the first aid kit too."

"Good plan," I said.

"You're bleeding all over the floor!" Vangie yelled. She too had headed into the living room to investigate the new commotion. I walked into the kitchen. Other than Emma, nobody else had noticed my presence.

Joe stood with one hand inside my tree, holding it up. Matty sat on my ottoman, holding his bleeding foot. Emma's boyfriend's face held a familiar expression of horror reserved for newbies to Leary clan gatherings. He was cute. Sandy-haired. Overdressed in a pair of dress slacks and a button-down shirt and tie. I guessed Joe and Matty planned to eat him alive.

Thunderous footsteps came down the stairs. My niece Jessa burst into the living room, hands on her hips. Lord. If it was possible, the kid had grown even since I'd seen her two weeks ago.

She thrust her face toward her mother's. "Am I ugly enough for you all now?"

"Cut the drama," Vangie said, as if it weren't part of her birthright.

"You're just ugly enough," Joe teased, peering around the side of the tree.

The door opened behind me and a blast of cold came in. This finally got the attention from the rest of the group. They all turned around as I did.

Jeanie came in wearing a Santa hat and carrying a green bag filled to the brim with presents.

"Ho, ho ho!" she said.

"Jeanie!" Jessa squealed. She ran to Jeanie and practically tackled her with a bear hug. I laughed as she blew right past me. Jeanie was always everyone's favorite.

"Cass!" Vangie said. "My God. You're here! How did you ... there's a blizzard. They're saying on the news the entire northern half of the state is shut down."

I smiled as my younger sister came to me and hugged me.

"Call it a Christmas miracle. I'll explain later. Everything smells delicious. When do we eat?"

"Two thousand and never," Matty said. "She's been futzing around in that kitchen for hours."

"Have you helped?" I asked. "Or have you just been storming in and out bitching about it?"

"Exactly," Vangie said. "Thank God I have reinforcements."

I went to Jeanie and took the present bag from her. My brothers would have done it but one of them was holding up the tree, the other one was busy bleeding out on my living room floor.

Emma reappeared with the broom, dust mop, and a box of bandages. While Emma tended to her uncle's wounds, I went to the tree.

"Just hold still," I told Joe. I got on my knees and felt around until I found the trunk. It had twisted in the base. I turned it and tightened the screws on the tree stand.

"There," I said. "Good as new."

"It's a menace," Joe said. "Might as well just light the thing on fire."

"The night is young," I said. He let go of the tree. I stood up and hugged him before he could make a clean getaway.

"Glad you made it back," he said. "I was starting to get worried. And how the hell did you manage to get back here?"

I smiled. "Had a little help."

"Did the reindeer fly you back?" Matty teased.

This got a laugh out of me. "Something like that." I looked out the kitchen window. I could see the lights on in the apartment above the garage but Nick hadn't yet come down.

"You look beautiful," I said to Jessa. She came to me and I got my hug. Emma had just finished wrapping Matty's wounded foot. He took a seat next to Tori on the couch.

"Oh, Aunt Cass, this is Robert," Emma said.

Robert rose to his feet. He was tall. Extremely so. He had to be at least six foot four and muscle-bound. I caught Joe's eye. He gave me a "don't even say it" look.

I shook Robert's hand and mouthed to my sister behind him.

"Do we like this one?"

Vangie shrugged. She went to the kitchen and opened the oven.

"All right, you mongrels," she said. "Set the table."

"Oh," I said. "About that. We're going to need to set an extra place."

Nobody asked me for whom. It was a Leary family rule. We had our own brand of chaos, but all were welcome here on the holidays. Jessa and Emma set about grabbing the plates and silverware. Joe came back from the garage and brought in an extra folding chair. Matty hobbled over to the closet under the stairs and pulled out the extra leaf for my table. Robert made himself useful helping Matty fit it in.

I got the serving spoons and the napkins. Within five minutes, we had the table ready. Vangie put the giant ham at the end of the table where Joe would sit. He was our designated carver.

"You sure it's a good idea to give Drunkle Joe a knife?" Jessa asked. Emma burst out laughing. Joe gave his daughter a withering look.

Jeanie walked in with the casserole dish filled with yams. "Glad you made it," she said to me. "Did you all hear? Your sister sprung Santa Claus out of jail!"

"I read about that," Emma said. "Great job, Aunt Cass. Sounds like your client's on the nice list."

"It was nothing," I said, smiling. "Just consider me another one of his happy elves."

"Aunt Cass saved Christmas," Jessa said. "I guess that sounds about right."

"Ho, ho, ho!" Nick Whittaker's booming voice filled the room.

Jessa turned. Her jaw dropped. So did mine. I'd seen the videos of Nick in his full regalia. I'd seen him from a distance across the street during the light show last night. A picture or two. But to see him up close, his full white beard, rosy cheeks, bulging middle, the brilliant red, white, and gold trim of his suit. Well, he was Santa Claus.

"Merry Christmas! Happy Holidays!" he said.

"Um ... everyone? I'd like you to meet ..."

"Santa himself!" Jeanie finished for me. Jessa was thirteen, far past believing. And yet, wonder filled her eyes.

Nick walked in carrying his own green velvet sack of presents. This must have been what he had stuffed into those lawn bags in the truck. As my entire family stared open-mouthed at him, Nick took small gifts out one by one and passed them out.

"Have you been naughty or nice?" he said to Matty.

"Well ..." Tori started.

"He's nice!" Jessa said. Like her mother, Jessa championed Matty at all costs.

"That's what I heard," Nick said.

"Uh ... we made you milk and cookies," Emma said. "We usually put them on a plate above the fireplace so the dogs don't get them."

"Where are the dogs, by the way?" I asked. I just then realized Marbury and Madison, my two adorable mutts, didn't herald my arrival with their usual barking and face licking.

"They've been making a habit sleeping in the other room with the baby," Tori said. "It's the cutest thing."

Matty put two fingers to his lips and let out a whistle. Two seconds later, the dogs came barreling around the corner. Madison slipped rounding the curve, but it didn't seem to slow her down. Marbury screeched to a halt as he took in the giant stranger in the red suit. But he recovered quickly and licked his nose as Nick bent down to pet him.

Nick reached into his bag and pulled out two rawhide treats, giving one to each pooch.

"Ho, ho, ho!" Another booming male voice came from the direction of the front door.

I froze as a second, much skinnier Santa stood there with his own sack of presents.

"What. Is. Happening?" Joe said. He stood at the end of the table, carving knife in hand. My heart raced.

"Eric!" I ran to the front door and threw my arms around him. "What are you doing here? You're supposed to be in North Carolina with your folks!"

"I ... uh ... wanted to surprise you. They decided to take a Christmas Caribbean cruise at the last minute." Eric and Nick sized each other up. Eric slowly slipped off his Santa hat, ceding to Nick's superiority.

"Set another plate," Vangie called out, unfazed by the new developments.

"Hope you came hungry," Jeanie said.

Just then, Santa #1's cell phone started to ring. He held up a gloved finger and excused himself into the other room.

"I'm so glad you're here," I said. Eric put an arm around me and kissed me.

"I didn't think we'd see you until at least tomorrow," he said. "The roads are shut down."

"Um ... my ride has a truck with a plow. And he knew the back roads," I said.

"Food's gonna get cold!" Vangie said. "We'll do presents later. Let's eat!"

We all took our places around the table. Joe said grace. As he finished, Nick walked back in, his eyes misted with tears.

"Is everything all right?" I asked. He nodded wordlessly. Jeanie pulled a chair out for him. Nick sunk into it.

"What is it?"

"Steve Anspaugh," he said. "That was Trudy, his wife. She ... she wanted to call and apologize. But ... Steve's awake. Cass, he's awake. He's talking. She says the doctors told her this could happen. It did. He's got a long, long road to recovery ahead of him. But he's talking! He knows who Trudy is. He's asking coherent questions. He ... he even asked to see me. He knows. He remembers I'm not the one who hurt him."

"Thank God," I said. "Oh, Nick. That's wonderful news."

"Answered prayers," Jeanie said.

"Dig in," Joe said as everyone started passing dishes around.

Eric squeezed my knee under the table. Then he leaned over and kissed me again. "Merry Christmas, Cass. Having you home safe is the only present I wanted." I kissed him back.

The food was delicious. The company was perfect. Nick couldn't stop himself from crying tears of joy. He was free. Steve Anspaugh was on the mend. And new, perfect snow started to fall, turning the lake into a wintry marvel.

Chapter 32

THE NEXT MORNING, Nick left early. I invited him to spend the day with us but he wanted to be with his own family for Christmas dinner. He thanked me again.

"Whenever you're in Helene, you've got a place to stay," he said. "We'd love to have you. I think the town kind of wants to adopt you. Aimee called and said people have been asking about you. They're grateful that you could help me."

"I'm grateful I could too," I said. "Drive safely. Text me when you make it back. And you have an open invitation to stay here too. I think the people of Delphi would love to meet you."

"I might just take you up on that. I'd like to see this lake in the summer. I've always wanted to learn how to water ski."

"Joe's a great teacher," I said. Then I had a vision of Santa Claus in swimming trunks up on water skis. That was a sight I most definitely wanted to see. Nick said his goodbyes to everyone in the house. They'd all stayed the night. Another Leary holiday tradition. Everybody comes and nobody leaves.

Later, in our pajamas, we opened our gifts. Nick had done a surprisingly good job picking things out for the members of my family he hadn't even met. Fishing lures for my brothers. Comfy slippers for Jeanie. A makeup kit for Jessa. For me, a new leather portfolio with my name embossed in gold.

"How on earth did he know?" Vangie asked. She'd just opened her gift. A cast iron Dutch oven painted bright red. Our grandmother had one like it. Vangie had accidentally dropped the lid when she was a kid, shattering it.

"Did you tell him?" she asked.

I shook my head. "I didn't even know he was planning on bringing presents. Honest."

Jessa passed out her gifts. She made us all identical dishes in her ceramics class. My mouth dropped as I opened mine. They were an odd, oblong shape and each dish had a small painted flower at one tip that made the whole thing look ... well ... uncannily like a certain part of the female anatomy.

"Well, this is ..." Matty started. Before he could finish, I lobbed a couch pillow across the room at him and hit him squarely in the forehead. Joe turned positively purple, trying not to laugh.

"They're beautiful," I said. "Thank you. I know just what to ... er ... put in mine."

"Oh, I just bet you ..." This time, Emma hurled a pillow and hit her father in the nose.

Beside me, Eric started choking on his hand. Later, we'd order pizza. Another Leary family tradition. We had our big meal on Christmas Eve. Christmas Day was more low key ... well ... as low key as Learys could be. Tonight, we'd head to midnight mass.

While my nieces found trash bags and busied themselves cleaning up the carnage of wrapping paper, I walked outside with Eric. The snow had stopped for now. The sky was still pure white. You couldn't see the other side of the lake anymore.

"It's beautiful," he said. Joe shoveled a path all the way to the water. I wore a cardigan over my PJs, but was still chilled. Eric took his coat off and put it around my shoulders. He held a mug of coffee. The steam made curly qs in the air between us.

"It's perfect," I said, leaning against his warmth. "I never want to be anywhere else on Christmas."

"Did you like Helene?"

"It's beautiful too. I met a lot of really nice people. A few awful ones."

"What you did is amazing though, Cass. I don't know how you do what you do sometimes."

"You helped," I said. "Thank you."

He kissed me. A different kind of warmth flooded me. My brothers came out, followed by both dogs and Jessa.

Joe carried three ice fishing poles. Matty carried a bucket. Jessa brought up the rear with a tackle box. The three of them walked out onto the ice. In the distance, Matty had set up a shanty. I could see three or four others dotted along the lake.

I turned back and looked up at the house. Vangie and Jeanie were in the kitchen, setting things up for dinner later. Emma and Robert were lacing up ice skates. Tori and the baby had curled up by the fireplace and fallen asleep.

"Come on," Eric said. "I think Joe's got a pair of hockey skates in the garage that will fit me. We can't let the youngsters show us up."

"Youngsters?" I teased him. "Did you learn that word during the Depression, old man?"

A few minutes later, I laced up my own skates. Early this morning, Matty had come out and used the snow blower and a bucket of water to clear and smooth a perfect rink near the shoreline. By late afternoon, we'd have dozens of kids from all around the lake out there taking a turn. For now, it was just us.

Eric skated circles around me. Emma and Robert waltzed hand in hand at the corners. I went to the center and performed an awkward spin.

"Caught one!" I heard Jessa holler from the shanty in the distance. "He's huge!" My brothers shouted their approval.

Jeanie watched it all from the window, sipping her hot chocolate.

This was Christmas on Finn Lake. Peace and gratitude filled me. These people. Their chaos. Their imperfections. Their fierce love for each other. My fierce love for them. I knew I was the luckiest woman on earth.

HAVE YOU READ THEM ALL YET?

Get caught up with the Cass Leary Legal Thriller Series today!

What readers are saying...

"...like old school Grisham with a strong female lead..."

"Taut legal mystery that will keep you up and night turning the pages."

"Whatever Robin James writes, I'm going to read. These books are *that* good!"

Available for Kindle, Print, Hardover and Audio!

WANT to know how to nab a FREE novella in the Cass Leary series and see what these characters really look like? Turn the page for more information.

Newsletter Sign Up

Sign up to get notified about Robin James's latest book releases, discounts, and author news. You'll also get *Crown of Thorne* an exclusive FREE bonus prologue to the Cass Leary Legal Thriller Series just for joining. Find out what really made Cass leave Killian Thorne and Chicago behind. As an additional bonus, you'll get access to the Cass Leary Character Gallery, a fun look at what these characters look like in the mind of their creator.

Click to Sign Up

http://www.robinjamesbooks.com/newsletter/

About the Author

Robin James is an attorney and former law professor. She's worked on a wide range of civil, criminal and family law cases in her twenty-five year legal career. She also spent over a decade as supervising attorney for a Michigan legal clinic assisting thousands of people who could not otherwise afford access to justice.

Robin now lives on a lake in southern Michigan with her husband, two children, and one lazy dog. Her favorite, pure Michigan writing spot is stretched out on the back of a pontoon watching the faster boats go by.

Sign up for Robin James's Legal Thriller Newsletter to get all the latest updates on her new releases and get a free bonus scene from Burden of Truth featuring Cass Leary's last day in Chicago. http://www.robinjamesbooks.com/newsletter/

Also By Robin James

Cass Leary Legal Thriller Series

Burden of Truth

Silent Witness

Devil's Bargain

Stolen Justice

Blood Evidence

Imminent Harm

First Degree

Mercy Kill

Guilty Acts

Cold Evidence

Dead Law

The Client List

Seasonable Doubt

With more to come...

Mara Brent Legal Thriller Series

Time of Justice

Price of Justice

Hand of Justice

Mark of Justice

Path of Justice

Vow of Justice

Web of Justice

Shadow of Justice

With more to come...

Audiobooks by Robin James

Cass Leary Series

Burden of Truth

Silent Witness

Devil's Bargain

Stolen Justice

Blood Evidence

Imminent Harm

First Degree

Mercy Kill

Guilty Acts

Cold Evidence

Dead Law

The Client List

Seasonable Doubt

Mara Brent Series

Time of Justice

Price of Justice

Hand of Justice

Mark of Justice

Path of Justice

Vow of Justice

Web of Justice

Shadow of Justice